THE SIGHT OF SEA AND SPIRIT

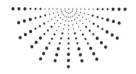

LACUNA REID

1
MIRA

I pull at one of the strands of red ribbon. The bow comes loose and slips away from the gift box. I reach for the lid and lift if off to reveal… *rose petals?*

God, Cliff, why do you have to be so creepy and symbolic… or whatever this is.

Everyone is watching; Theo, my tall, dark, and handsome architect; gorgeous Gino, with his light brown hair and green eyes; my beautiful blue-eyed Greek Elias; and wild, muscly Helio with his long, dark hair. They are all so important to me, and yet in this moment, my heart catches in my throat. *Am I important enough to them to withstand whatever it is my stalkerish ex is about to throw at us?*

I reach into the box and rustle through the petals, terrified that I might find something gross like an animal heart or a dead bird. In the end, all I find is another small box… another jewelry box. My heart sinks as I lift it up. There's an inevitability to all this, and I'm already sure what's inside, but I can't put it back. I can't hide it. It's too late. They are all here and they are about to find out my secret. I open the small black jewelry case to reveal a plain gold ring.

My wedding band.

The guys around me gasp and so does Marina, the office manager.

"Is this… is this a proposal?!" she cries, clasping her hands over her mouth. "Who is it from?" She looks around at the guys and they look at her and each other blankly.

"No," I say. "It's not a proposal. It's my wedding ring. I'm… married."

"You're… what?" Gino says.

"I mean… I'm separated. I was married to Cliff and then I left – five years ago. I walked out, and I haven't spoken to him since."

"It didn't cross your mind to file for divorce?" Helio teases, but I'm not in the mood.

"I don't want anything to do with that man," I say. "I didn't want to have to negotiate with him. Plus, I couldn't afford a lawyer to file for divorce. It was easier not to think about it."

"So, you want to stay married?" Theo asks me. There's pain and concern in his eyes.

"No. Not at all," I say. "Look… as far as I'm concerned, I'm no longer married to him, but…"

"But legally…" says Elias.

"Legally you are his wife," Theo says.

"I guess..." I look around the room at the guys. Marina seems to have quietly melted away into another room, giving us privacy. I'm glad because all their faces show some kind of pain and betrayal that they either can't mask or aren't trying to hide.

"Which means you can't marry any of us to get out of this immigration bind," Gino says, his eyes downcast, his voice distant. "That's too bad; it would have simplified things."

"But you can still sort it out... right?" I ask.

"I'll do my best, Mira," Gino says, "but this complicates things. We are trying to show that your life is here – but perhaps Clifford is telling them otherwise, perhaps his lawyers are getting in the way of your application because you are still his wife."

"I don't want to be," I say.

"Then file for divorce!" There's rage in Theo's voice, and even though I know it's probably not directed at me, it still feels that way. I flinch.

He notices. "I'm sorry, Mira," Theo says, looking down. "This is all a bit too much for me, on top of everything."

Theo just had to deal with his closest confidant trying to kill me... Victor was now in police custody, for the murder of fifteen-year-old Tiala many years ago. The danger might have passed for now, but we've all been through so much in the past twenty-four hours that this "gift" from my ex really couldn't have come at a worse time.

"It's too much to deal with now," I say. "Let's just all take a few days to relax." But even as I say it, my voice full of false cheer, I can see the darkness in the faces of these four men… I have developed strong feelings for all of them, and I've been demanding the truth from them, yet I've been keeping a secret, and I can tell they're hurt.

It wasn't a big deal for me, I tell myself as the guys make their excuses and disperse, leaving me standing here alone.

But that's not really true is it, Mira, another voice in my head says, sounding unnervingly like my mother who passed away when I was younger. *You'd like to think it's not a big deal, but really, you've been in denial this whole time and you need to stop running from yourself.*

2
THEO

"I'm married," Mira says… and something inside me breaks.

I have to leave.

But I stand here, feeling numb. I'm speaking, but the words that come out sound defensive. They sound like they have emotion, despite the fact that all I'm experiencing now is a swirling sensation in my gut, and a heaviness closing in on my mind.

I've made things wrong. I've used the wrong words, and Mira looks shocked.

I need to get away from her. I need to protect her from whatever's going on inside me while I process this news.

I retreat to my study.

It's usually a welcome escape to be here, alone, to look out the windows at everything I've created, but all of a sudden it feels worthless.

My confidence is shot, as if everything that I've been working for… that we've been working for all these years has been reduced to dust.

Why didn't Mira tell us?

She brushed it off just now as a technicality, as something in the past, but if so, why would she hide it from us?

I pace back and forth mulling it over.

I haven't been certain of anything more in my life than I was of her, and that started even before we met in this lifetime. It was my conviction that this was my destiny. It was my destiny to find Mira… to be with her, just as it was my destiny to know the others, and to come here and build El Cielo… and now that certainty has vanished, has crumbled, has been crushed by a ring and two words.

I'm on such shaky ground internally that I don't know what to do.

Surely there's more to this than Mira is talking about. Otherwise she would have been open from the start.

Is it possible that she was just going along with us for the ride, but that ultimately, she belongs to someone else?

She says she can't stand her ex, but he has this claim over her that she's never even sought to relinquish. It feels like some kind of twisted love story – star-crossed lovers – and we're just the guys in the way.

I can't help it.

I try to pour myself a glass of whiskey. But my hands are

shaking so much that it's knocked to the floor, shattering and casting shards of glinting glass across the room.

Before I can stop it, the emotion overtakes me and I break down, right down to my knees, and cry for the first time in decades

All my life I've yearned to be in control; I thirsted for authority. It was where I found my sense of self, despite a childhood of neglect, despite my parents never really giving a damn.

And yet in a moment, the rug has been pulled from beneath my feet. My ego... my career... my entire life... It all seems pointless if I can't have her... if we can't be together... if she belongs to someone else.

There's a knock at the door and I yell: "Go away."

I don't want anyone to see me like this, especially not her... but I hear the door open and Gino is there, not following my instructions, as usual.

"Let's go," he says, simultaneously ignoring the state that he's found me in, and also giving me the 'out' that I need.

Gino always seems to know exactly what to say.

I get up, wipe the tears from my eyes and follow him out of the room.

He's right.

We need to get out of here. We need to clear our heads. We need time to think.

3
MIRA

I go back to my rooms, feeling terrible. I was so young when I married Cliff... only 19, and I didn't know any better, not after the way my father had raised me. I unwittingly went from one controlling man to another. Cliff and my father are like two peas in a pod, both rich, business-minded, isolated, and power tripping.

I sprawl out on my bed and mope for a bit... feeling sorry for myself.

Now the guys don't trust me... and is that really because I didn't trust them?

I didn't tell them I was married. I didn't want to seem frumpy, like an old married lady... or old-fashioned in that frowned-upon marrying-at-nineteen kind of way.

I have the need to talk to someone, to vent about how I feel, but somehow, I don't feel like anyone here is on speaking terms with me. I briefly consider confiding in Marina. She seems nice, but really, I hardly know her. Instead, I reach for my phone and call Lana, my best friend who's back in New York, living nearby where I used to live. It strikes me that my old life in New York was only months ago... *it feels like years.*

The phone rings and Lana picks up.

"Finished your orgy?" she says. I'd forgotten that she had only just called me, a couple of hours ago, and I happened to be lying on a pile of mattresses with four sexy guys. That also feels like a long time ago.

"That wasn't what it looked like," I say.

Nothing had happened – sexually, not at that point. We had just all slept in Theo's study after Victor was finally apprehended. I'd not wanted to be apart from any of them and they'd not wanted to be away from me. It was special... it felt like a new level of something in our 'relationship' – if you can call it that, but of course Lana assumed we'd all been fucking.

"Sure, sure," Lana replies. "You know you don't have to hide your sultry slutty side from me. I'm here for it, especially now that you've sorted out your birth control."

Lana had been texting me and harassing me about birth control, and I finally made it to the local doctors to get an IUD, but I'd almost forgotten about that in the chaos of everything that happened in the past few days. I hadn't told the guys yet because I'm still not sure about where we stand relationship-wise.

"Come on," Lana says, "I want details. Let me live vicariously through you. Show some charity to those of us who are happily partnered with just one guy." Lana has been with Dave for a very long time. He's a sweetheart and she is happy, but she does keep asking me for details about the unusual romantic situation I've found myself in.

"I guess I better explain how it all happened." I tell Lana about the night we'd just had – about Tiala's ghost and Victor being the killer, and how the guys had helped and how we'd all ended up sleeping in Theo's study.

"Wow," Lana says. "That's so intense. Are you alright – given you were almost murdered!"

"I'm alright now…" I say.

"You should write a movie script about all that. Wait, what's wrong?" Lana asks, as if she's only noticed the sadness in my voice, and that I'm not really alright after all.

"It's Cliff," I say. "He sent me a box full of rose petals… and my wedding band."

"What. The. Fuck?"

"Exactly."

"That's creepy stalker material," Lana says. "You really should be writing a soap opera."

"It's not funny, Lana," I say. "The guys didn't know I was married, and it kind of… it makes things weird."

"That's not fair," Lana says. "You were practically a child bride. Did you tell them that?"

"No, because it's not true," I say.

"You were so innocent!" Lana argues. "It's totally true."

"I think it's mostly the fact that I didn't tell them that's bothering them, and also… there are some immigration issues. Gino thinks Cliff is behind it with his lawyers – sabotaging my being here... maybe me still being legally married means that Cliff can argue that my life's not really here and I shouldn't have longer term residency, or something."

"That's fucked," Lana says. "I'm sorry, honey."

It feels good to get her empathy.

"So even if the guys do know that my marriage doesn't mean anything to me, it's getting in the way on a practical level, and it also means one of them can't marry me to help me stay in the country."

"Wow – that developed fast," Lana says. "You'd really do that?"

"It doesn't mean anything, does it?" I ask. "It's just a piece of paper saying you're legally connected."

"So romantic," Lana says, sarcastically. "You know, it's not fair that someone like you is getting all the romance. It's totally wasted on you."

"Shut up," I say.

"I would shut up, but then I wouldn't be able to tell my best friend some important news about my life, that is – if she's not too wrapped up in her own to care." Lana is joking, but there's an edge to her voice. She's pouting at me, as if she's upset that I've neglected her recently.

"I'm sorry," I say. "What is it?"

Lana holds up her hand to reveal a sapphire ring on her wedding finger.

"No way!" I say. "Dave proposed?"

"Finally," Lana says. "I was about to give up on him and just do it myself."

"Congrats, honey!" I say. "I really am happy for you."

"Good, then you can be my bridesmaid."

"I'd be honored… ummm… when's the wedding?" I ask.

"Oh, probably not for years. It took him this long to propose, I can't imagine he's in a rush."

"Keep me in the loop," I say. "And I really am thrilled for you!"

"Of course," Lana says, smiling at me. "Look, I'd better go, but you'll keep me in the loop, too. Let me know what happens. I'm always here if you need someone to chat to.

"Thanks, Lana."

We exit the phone call, and I lie back on my bed again, feeling better somehow. I know I need to make things right with the guys. I need to talk to them one-on-one, and make sure they understand that me being married doesn't mean anything to me… that it doesn't change anything between us.

4

MIRA

I get out of bed and shower, and then I go to my wardrobe, eyeing the nice things that Theo generously gave me. I put on a fairly casual looking top. It's cream linen, and it feels expensive, but I pair it with my worn blue jeans anyway because I'm not in a fancy mood.

I pile my hair up into a messy bun and put on my sneakers, and then I go in search of my four kind-of-boyfriends. I don't really know what to call them. We haven't talked about official titles, but there's definitely some kind of relationship between me and each of them, although after the shock this morning, I'm worried that one or more of them will have changed their minds about wanting to be close to me.

I try Theo's office first. His outburst this morning did put me on edge, but it's so uncharacteristic of him. I want to make sure he's okay. There's no answer when I knock on his door. I pause for a while and then continue across to the main building to Gino's apartment. I press the buzzer, but there's no response there either… how mysterious. I go downstairs to the lobby.

Marina smiles at me, through her long eyelashes. With her beautiful caramel curls, she always looks perfectly groomed, and despite my shower this morning, I'm still feeling disheveled.

"Tough day?" she says.

I sigh. "How did you guess?" I say with a touch of irony in my voice.

"Gino and Theo left earlier if you're looking for them," Marina informs me.

"Where…?"

"They didn't say," she replies before I even finish answering the question.

I eye her suspiciously, not sure whether to trust her.

"Look, Mira," she says. "I know we don't know each other very well, but I like you, and I want you to know that whatever is going on between you and the guys, there's no judgement from me, okay?"

I smile weakly. "Okay. Thanks," I say, and I mean it. I might not really be in a smiley mood, but it's sweet of her to go to the trouble to put me at ease.

"Things seem complicated," she says. "I'm not going to ask you for details, but I just want you to know that I'm here for you if you need me."

"Thanks…" I say. "Umm, did you… did you hear…"

"About Victor?" Marina fills in. "Yes, Gino told me. What a creep. You know I always thought there was something wrong there. I could never understand why Theo kept him around, but I never suspected anything like that."

"I guess none of us did," I say.

"You've been through a lot, huh?" Marina says. "Hey, if you like, we could have coffee together sometime. I make a mean latte."

"That sounds nice," I say, smiling more warmly this time.

I say goodbye to Marina and head out through the main doors, and into the forest. I'm looking for the pathway to Helio's hut, I can't remember where it is. Then I hear the hammering sound that I've heard him make before and follow it.

Helio is back in the first place I ever ran in to him out here in the forest, smashing a mallet against the same spot. His muscular body gleams with sweat. He's only wearing a singlet and shorts, not leaving much to the imagination, but my mind goes there anyway, imagining that I'm the one he's pounding all his strength into. *Mmmmm.*

"Fixing the water pump again?" I ask.

Helio turns towards me, as if he knew I was there all along – as if he was expecting me. His face spreads into a slow smile.

"This damn thing always breaks," he says, gesturing to the spot where he was hammering. "The aluminum comes loose around here." Then Helio looks back at me. "How can I help you, princess?"

"So, I'm back to being a princess again, am I?"

"What would you prefer I call you?" Helio asks, and this time there's a note of earnestness in his voice, as if he's concerned he might have offended me. I'm used to Helio being all arrogance and cocky charm. I'm not used to him being concerned about something small like this.

"I don't know." I shrug. "I guess most things would be better than 'princess'."

"Noted," Helio says, and turns back towards the water pump to appraise his work.

"Helio, I'm sorry," I say. "I should have told you I was married. I didn't think it was important... I mean, it was a long time ago and Cliff's not in my life anymore." *...well, not if I can help it anyway.*

"No need to apologize to me, Mira... *está bien*; it's fine. Save your apologies for the others, they might care more."

"You don't care?" I say and the words cut into me as they fly out of my mouth... I must be feeling sensitive after the ordeal. I shake myself. *Of course, I'm feeling sensitive. I was almost murdered.* It's still so surreal and I don't know how to integrate all that into my normal experience of life.

"Hey, hey, not like that..." Helio says, his voice gentle. He steps towards me, looking as if he wants to hug me, but stops. It's either because he remembers he's not a cuddler, or he just realizes how sweaty he is. "I mean – your marital status is nothing to me. I don't believe in marriage."

"Neither do I," I say, relieved. Although there's a feeling of disappointment too, as if there's a small surprising part of me that wants Helio to want me so much that he suddenly does believe in marriage… it's ridiculous, but it's there.

"Hah – if anything it's kind of sexy," Helio says. "Fucking a married woman…"

"You're definitely not the romantic type," I say, half turned-on, half repulsed, by his flippant remark.

"What would you know?" he says defensively.

"I… I didn't mean to offend you," I say softly.

Helio shrugs. "This isn't easy for me, Mira. I'm trying not to be an arsehole. Honestly, I'm trying, but you bring out these feelings in me…"

His voice is almost breaking under the weight of his emotion.

"It's okay," I say.

"I… I better get back to this," Helio says, and it's obvious he needs some time alone.

As I turn to walk away, Helio speaks again.

"I'm always up for a re-match of what we did at the lake… anytime."

"Sure," I say, remembering the blinding orgasms and the mind-blowing sex… "but…"

"Yeah, I know," Helio says. "Next time, don't fuck and run. I get it."

I smile as I walk away, relieved that Helio does seem to be getting it, at last, and meanwhile, I'm wanting more… much more.

5
MIRA

I walk back towards the main buildings of El Cielo. There's something hauntingly beautiful about them, and about this place – the way the vines grow up the sides of the old silos that have been converted from the futurist 1930s concrete factory with its elegant arched Spanish gothic windows into Theo's architectural masterpiece – an overgrown post-industrial fairy-land.

As soon as I'm inside again, my senses are permeated by the strong scent of citrus. I follow it through the baroque dining hall and into the kitchen. I remember the first time Theo showed me around El Cielo and how I fell in love with the place, especially the enormous kitchen with its stone benches and brass fittings; it's bigger than some of the restaurant kitchens I've cheffed in, and yet so much more elegant.

I can tell as soon as I enter that, of course, it's Elias who's responsible for the citrus scent. I see him at one of the center benches, surrounded by lemons. He's slicing them in half and stuffing them into jars.

"Making preserved lemons?" I ask.

Elias is startled by my voice. He looks up at me with his dark blue eyes and messy black hair; there's a vulnerability in his expression I'm not used to.

"Yes," he says, and keeps slicing.

"Elias, I'm sorry."

Even though he's clearly not happy with me, I enjoy the sight of him – his lean, muscular build, the gorgeous symmetry of his face, his perfectly tanned skin… Seeing him here preserving is almost too hot, but clearly, he's not in the mood… *yet*.

I take a deep breath, enjoying the citrussy aromas, and wait for him to respond.

"Mira," he says, eventually. "It's… it's just that after this morning, when I found out you were married, I was hit with… unexpected emotion."

"Oh?"

"I just had this feeling that you were going to leave," Elias says, his eyes glistening with tears. "It… it reminded me of when I was a little boy and we got the news about my mother's cancer."

Ouch…

"I had no idea," I say.

"But are you…?" Elias says. "Are you going to leave us?" and in his tone I can hear that little boy. My heart breaks for him.

"Not if I can help it," I reply, stepping toward Elias. "I love it here… and… I love you."

It might be a bit premature to say, but for some reason it feels right. Of course, I love Elias. I love everything about him, from his sweetness and sensuality to his gorgeous body, to his love of food…

A different expression takes over his handsome face – pure joy – and if any smile could light up the world, it would be his right now.

"You… love me?" he says, enthusiastically sweeping me up in his arms, kissing me gently, passionately.

"Of course, I do," I say to Elias. "I have for many lifetimes."

"And of course, I love you too, Mira… for many lifetimes."

His words send a blissful jolt though my heart. It feels so good to hear it – to be loved, and to know it. I lean into Elias, breathing him in, the smell of citrus and herbs… I could get high on this scent… *it feels like I am high already.*

"I apologize, Mira," Elias says, raising his hands. "I seem to have coated you in citrus."

I giggle. "I don't mind," I say. "It's kind of sexy."

Elias takes a deep breath pulling me close, and I can feel his desire for me.

"Is anyone likely to come in here?" I ask.

"No, It's Calista's day off and there are no functions today, so there are no kitchen helpers around."

"Well, in that case, I have a request,"

Elias looks at me, his blue eyes gleaming mischievously. "What is it you want, *latria mu?*"

I look up at Elias and I can't stop myself from doing everything I can to fulfil my own desires.

"I want you to take me… to make love to me right now… right here."

Elias' eyes widen in surprise. "Here?"

"Here, on the kitchen bench," I say, trying to keep my voice even and low, even though it threatens to leap up to a high pitch in my excitement. I've fantasized about this so many times and I'll be damned if I'm not going to make the most of this opportunity.

Elias sighs in pleasure and desire, he pulls me close, holds me tight, and whispers, "as you wish."

He kisses me deeply, his big hands caressing my breasts under the linen fabric of my shirt. Then he reaches for the buttons, undoing them, exposing my chest.

"Oh, Mira," Elias says, admiring me and the good cleavage provided by this excellent bra I'm wearing – one that Theo bought me. He leans down and presses his face between my breasts, breathing me in for a moment. Then he groans in pleasure, wraps his arms firmly underneath me and quickly hoists me up onto the bench. My stomach flips at the sudden movement.

Elias sweeps aside the lemons from behind me on the bench and reaches for the button of my jeans, then he pauses.

"Are you sure you want this?" he asks.

"Yes," I say, reaching for him and pulling him into a kiss.

"I don't have protection," Elias says.

"Oh," I say. "Neither do I… wait, umm…" This feels slightly

awkward, but I probably should have had this conversation with the guys by now. "I mean... have you been tested lately? Are you clean?"

"Yes," Elias says. "But..."

"I'm on contraceptives," I say, thinking of the IUD implanted inside me which, in itself is not the sexiest thought.

"Mira..." Elias says, his eyes widening... "I..."

"I want to feel you... inside me... just you, with no barriers," I say.

"But... I don't usually... outside of a relationship..." Elias blushes.

Something churns inside me, good and bad and painful and delicious.

"Do you want to be in a relationship with me, Elias?" I ask.

"Yes... but..."

I kiss him again, more deeply and passionately then before pulling him up against the bench, close enough that his magnificent erection grinds against my mound. Then I release him.

"The thing is..." I say. "I can be committed to you, I really can – but only if there's a possibility of me still being with the others too, with Theo, Gino, Helio... I have feelings for all of you. Please don't make me choose."

Elias contemplates this for a moment, then he looks deep into my eyes. "That's as it should be, my love," he says. Then his hands are all over me, slipping my shirt off, unhooking my bra, caressing my breasts, grabbing my ass, undoing the buttons on my jeans and tugging them off, along with my panties.

Elias pushes me back, gently, laying me down on the bench. I find myself naked in the middle of the kitchen, surrounded by citrus. I feel the lemon juice, spilled from Elias' preserving efforts, sticky and tingly on my skin.

Elias pauses for a moment, taking me in, then he runs his hands, gently, all over my body, making me sigh and groan in pleasure, before lowering his face to my pussy. His tongue feels so good as it slips between my lips and hovers over my clit. Then Elias devours me, as if he's famished and I'm the most delicious meal he's ever feasted upon, growling like a dog with a bone, sending vibrations shivering through me across my body. I'm close to the edge, but I want him to fill me so I push him back, by the shoulders and reach for his fly. I don't have time to take off the rest of his clothes because my need is so urgent… *right now.*

Elias' enormous cock swings free of his boxers. He looks down with an amused expression on his face, seeing me fully naked and himself almost fully clothed, and sensing my urgent need for him, and noting the kitchen bench is exactly the right height for this… for my tall Greek god to impale me with his enormous cock.

"Mira…" he whispers, as I pull him towards me, into me.

He enters me slowly, filling me up inside… the feeling is like warm honey… pouring into me, oozing through me. Sweet and tender and delicious as it fills me right up.

Then Elias gives into his passion. He moans and grabs my

ass. He thrusts into me, faster this time. His hard cock feels delicious inside me. He pulls back and thrusts again, even deeper, making me groan in pleasure as his sizeable cock hits my sweet spot. Elias pulls back, his eyes shining as if he's mesmerized by the sight of me.

I writhe on the bench, sticky, and wanting more. I grab him by the butt cheeks and pull him in.

Elias loses all semblance of control as his desire takes over and he thrusts into me again, and again.

There's a slight pause in momentum and Elias has a glint in his eye. Then he hoists my legs up around his hips, wraps my arms around his neck, and with god-like strength lifts us both up, even higher into the center of the bench, sending more lemons tumbling to the floor.

"I'll pick them up later," he says, taking off his t-shirt and throwing it down towards the lemons on the ground. His skin feels so good against me, inside me…

Elias hitches my hips and thrusts deeper into me – filling me up to the point of bursting, ploughing a pleasurable pain through me. I reach up and claw against his chest, leaving scratches and eliciting another groan. He pumps harder and faster into me, sending me right to the edge and I come – spiraling into outer space. I'm not just seeing stars and sparkles – this is an all-out hallucination. I'm seeing magnolia petals cascading around us, and lemon blossoms and autumn leaves… I'm seeing the face of God… who looks an awful lot like Micah… who I used to think of as my childhood imaginary friend, but who I now know is a kind of guardian angel or spirit guide... I'm seeing the birth of the world, the explosion of the big bang, the sunrise... *Oh. My. Gods...*

Elias moans, and thrusts one last time, emptying himself into me.

We lie here, sweaty and blissful... high on our sex, on our endorphins, on each other. An eternity might as well have passed because time has stopped and I've been to heaven and back in the last few minutes... but even an eternity is too soon.

Eventually Elias pulls out and grabs his t-shirt. He passes it to me to put between my legs and soak up his mess. It's all a bit of a mess. I'm sticky and lemony... my hair has come undone and it feels weird to put on my clothes.

"Don't worry about the mess," Elias says, winking at me. "I'll clean it up."

I smile and thank him. I'm not really clean enough to be cleaning right now.

"I think I better go shower again," I say... "Or take a nice long soak in the tub."

"Mmm," Elias hums into my neck, pulling me close, and interrupting me as I struggle to re-clothe myself. "I wish I could have a bath with you, but I better tidy this up and finish my preserving." He looks a bit sheepish, as if I might tell him off for his hygiene practices.

"I'm sure you'll wipe everything down properly," I say, nudging him.

"If you want me..." Elias says, causing another jolt of desire to course through to my groin even though I thought I was spent. "...anytime, all you need to do is call."

"Thank you," I say, giving him a quick kiss. "I will."

"I mean it," Elias says, holding me firmly in his arms. "I don't want to crowd you, Mira. I know you've got a lot… going on. You just tell me what you need and I'll be there – even if it's just someone to hold you at night."

"Thanks," I say again, and I really mean it. Elias must be just about the sweetest man alive, and here he is, offering me anything I want, even though he's clearly not the only guy I'm involved with, and the others all happen to be his best friends in the world. How did my life come to be so… *so freaking AMAZING!?*

We say our sweet sticky goodbyes, and I take my disheveled self discretely up to my room right away to get cleaned up. I run a bath and strip off the clothes that were clean only a couple of hours ago. I pour fancy bubble bath that smells like roses into the tub and then I stand and look at myself in the mirror. I look… *normal.* Just like a normal human being, not like the goddess that the guys seem to think I am.

They treat me like I'm a super model or something, like I'm special, not just for how I look but for who I am, and I guess that is just what we are to each other… special… and what we have been for many lifetimes.

I feel a sudden pang of longing to unravel the mystery of this place – El Cielo – and how it seems to have brought us together again… and to find out why we seem to be doing this, coming together, life after life… *what does it all mean?*

Maybe some of the books on Theo's enormous bookshelves have some answers, some clues, as to what's going on here and what the deeper purpose is, because there must be some reason… it can't possibly just be chance. It's too much of a coincidence.

I get into the tub, with my Kindle, careful not to get it wet. The water swells up around me, soothing me. I relax back, letting out a sigh, surrendering myself to the soothing heat. I flick my Kindle on to the new reverse harem book I downloaded. The term itself used to be enough to make me blush but now I find myself in a similar situation and these books are the closest thing I have to dating advice. The book I'm reading is the first in the Nevermore Bookshop series, by Steffanie Holmes. It's described as a paranormal romance that's kind of like the Black Books TV show, crossed with Agatha Christie novels. I'm a big fan of the show and I love a good murder mystery, so I was sold straight away… also, I figure, since no one I know in the real world can give me advice on how to have multiple boyfriends, I might as well learn what I can from fictional stories while enjoying myself at the same time – not that I officially have multiple boyfriends…. yet, but it's certainly part of my plan. I quickly lose myself in the engrossing story.

6
MIRA

My soak in the tub is so relaxing that I feel like a real-life princess, bringing home the fact that my life has been a strangely beautiful fairy tale recently, if a little haunting (literally), and way too scary for my liking. It still feels weird to be alone after Victor's attack. I have half a mind to take Elias up on his perennial offer of cuddles and invite him into my bed for the night.

Eventually I get out of the tub and wander around in a fluffy white towel for a while, feeling a bit dazed. I finally managed to slip on my purple silk pajamas when there's a knock at the door. I freeze instinctively, and then realize it's probably one of the guys I call out, "Who's there?"

"Hello, Mira," Theo's voice says through the door. "I don't mean to disturb you… but I'm wondering if I can have a word."

I let him in.

Theo takes in the sight of me in the sleepwear he chose; he seems to lose his train of thought and stares for a moment longer than usual before he pulls himself together.

"Mira," he says, looking as if he'd rather be doing something else, other than talking… something very specific that involves being approximately two meters closer, and all over me. The thought sends a shiver of pleasure through me and I reach out my hand towards him. He steps forward and takes my hand, in response.

"I came here to apologize," he said. "I'm sorry for my outburst, earlier. I was shocked…"

"Yeah, I know," I say. "It's fine, really… I mean, you startled me, but I get it."

"It was a crushing blow to me," Theo continues, "… to know that you are still legally wed to that man…"

"Well…"

"Do you…" Theo starts and then stops and starts again. "I meant what I said, earlier, despite my tone being inappropriate."

"You mean, about divorce?" I ask.

"Yes," Theo says. "Do you want a divorce? I'm here to support you, truly. I can offer you the best lawyers – whatever you want… unless…"

Theo lowers his gaze.

"What?"

"Unless you are still holding onto Clifford Maxwell, and that is why you're still married," Theo says.

His words are sharp – and feel like an accusation, but it's clear this is what he's been fearing.

"You think that my marital status means something to me?" I ask, it comes out in a laugh, and that seems almost as inappropriate as my words suddenly sound. "I'm sorry…" I say, trying to make myself make sense.

"Perhaps your life here is just a phase to you," Theo says, letting go of my hand and stepping away.

He begins to pace the room. "Perhaps this is just a passing fling and you want to go back to him."

It's my turn to snap.

"No!"

Theo stops pacing, and faces me.

I realize there are tears running down my cheeks and Theo swoops in towards me, cradling me in his arms, whispering soothing sounds in my ear. "There, there."

Theo's voice is usually sexy, but now, as a low, horse whisper…. it's irresistible.

"I honestly want nothing to do with Cliff," I say into Theo's shoulder. "That's why I never contacted him to ask for a divorce."

"You needed to ask him?"

I nod. "Divorce laws in New York are kind of archaic – unless you both agree to divorce you need to go through a whole messy process of proving the other person is at fault. I knew he wouldn't be amicable about it. I didn't even want to ever see him again. I haven't spoken to him since before the day he left. He was overseas and I just walked out. I expected him to come after me, but he never did. I don't think he expected me to survive in the real world."

"What do you mean?" Theo asks, looking puzzled.

"Cliff kept me in a cage, just like my father before him. I bet he thought I'd get burned out and come back to him… I bet that's why he never came after me, he was just waiting until he had all the power again. I was terrified he'd track me down…"

Theo looks down at me with his deep brown eyes, his eyebrows crease in concern. "He hurt you?"

"It's hard to explain," I say, leaning more deeply into Theo as he strokes my hair. "He hurt me in so many ways, but not the ways you'd expect… I'm still processing it – all of it… my father was the same."

There's anger in Theo's eyes as I speak.

"It was a *kind* of abuse," I say "– not that they hit me, they threatened to. They just controlled every move I made, everything I did; they locked me away… My father would lock me in the fucking wardrobe when I was a kid. It was terrifying."

"I'm sorry, Mira," Theo says, stepping away and taking my hands.

"What for?" I ask.

"The blindfolds – that must have been what went wrong, why you cried."

"Oh…" I say, recalling the incident that started off incredibly sexy – with Theo tying me blindfolded to his bed with silk ties, and ended with me in a blubbering mess. "I think it must have triggered something." I say.

"It won't happen again, I promise," Theo says.

"No – Theo…" I struggle to find the words to express myself. "It's what I want," I tell him. "I've been doing some research. I've read a few articles on how kink play – bondage, and domination – can be therapeutic. I think… I think that it might be a way for me to heal, but only if it's done properly, safely."

Theo considers my words for a moment.

"You want me to learn?" he asks. His voice takes on an unusual tone and I'm not sure if it's in pleasure or pain or perhaps both. Then it drops back into a coarse whisper. "You want me to learn to tie you up properly…" Theo croons into my neck and I feel tingles in all the right places.

"Mmm hmmm," I croon back, melting into Theo.

"Nothing would please me more," he says. There is hunger in his eyes. He holds me tighter and tells me I smell like roses. He kisses me passionately, and then he leaves me wanting.

Theo has to leave; he says he has some urgent business to attend to and part of me is hoping the urgent business is actually researching bondage practices. I lock the door behind him, still not a hundred percent sure I want to be alone, but after everything I've been through in the past few days, my brain is foggy and exhausted. I go to bed, and fall quickly to sleep.

7

MYA

*T*he night air is heavy with anticipation. We prepare the temple, sweeping it with special brooms made of reeds, mixing the sacred oils, burning bundles of herbs, and chanting. This is where the Mysteries will take place. I don't know much about them. No one seems to, even those who have participated before. I know this is no ordinary temple rite. It's even more secret than the Great Rite. I know there is a special potion involved.

Alesia told us that the potion enables the gods to inhabit our bodies, just for the evening, and that we cannot be held responsible for the will of the gods. There are rumors that the potion makes people sick, that it makes them lose their minds. I asked Alesia what it's made from. She told me it's to do with the grains favored by Dionysus, that he blesses the grains with his own special ambrosia. I'm so curious I had to bite my tongue to stop further questions. I *didn't want to get on Alesia's bad side and I had the feeling she didn't have any more to say than that.*

From what Alesia said, it sounds like a party – a party that the gods are invited to, and they take our bodies to get there. So strange.

Just as I finish sweeping the corner of the temple that I've been allocated, I catch a glimpse of Amedes. He stands close to Alesia, his hand brushing hair from her shoulder. I feel a pang of jealousy even though I have no claim over him. I can't hear the conversation, but Alesia smiles at him and embraces him. I can tell there is something between them, or maybe there was and it's just the memory that lingers. I suppose I can't judge when I've been fantasizing about almost every man I've laid eyes on recently.

I expect the night to go more like the Great Rite, but after the incense and bundles of herbs have burned out, they are cleared away and baskets of fruit are brought to the altar, dripping with grapes and glistening with pomegranates. Other platters of all kinds of food that we don't normally eat at the temple follow them, roasted ducks and oxen legs, feta and olives, among an array of honeyed vegetables and unusual breads. We normally eat such simple food here – plain vegetables, beans and grains – that my mouth is watering. I hope the gods are to partake in this feast through us, and that we get to taste everything even though they are in control. Wine is brought out too, and I recognize the honey wine gifted by my family among the other vessels of grape wine. They must have been saving it all for a special occasion.

We go to the chambers to prepare. Unlike the last ritual, where all the other priestesses were serious and solemn, this time they're giggling and smiling, but none of them would tell me why. "It's a mystery... you'll see," they said. Excitement sizzles in the air as we wash and oil ourselves. This time, instead of the white ritual robes, Alessa produces a giant sack filled with colorful bundles.

"Close your eyes," she says, "and pull out whichever bundle comes first."

I watch as the other priestesses draw out bundles and smile at the colors they receive: different shades of green, blue, purple, yellow, and red.

"Don't unwrap them just yet," Alessa tells us. "Wait until they've all been drawn. Don't spoil the surprise for the new priestesses."

When it's my turn, I draw out a turquoise bundle, and after a few more moments, we're permitted to unwrap them.

I sigh as the robes unfold in waves of turquoise and silver. They're the most beautiful clothing I've ever seen. Something hard is lodged in the center of them and I retrieve it from in between the folds.

"It's a mask!" I say, more to myself than to the others. They laugh around me, showing me their masks, too. The masks all seem to match the robes, meaning mine is turquoise and gold.

"The masks belong to your patron goddesses for the evening," Alessa says.

She steps towards me, lowering her voice, "Turquoise is one of the colors associated with Artemis."

Alessia continues around the group of priestesses as we dress, quietly informing them which goddess they are to be taking the form of for the night.

"Artemis had many lovers," the dark-haired priestess next to me says, and winks.

I blush.

Cold dread and hot anticipation wind their way through my guts and up into my chest, heavy and light at the same time. I want to run away almost as much as I want to run towards whatever is coming. I shiver under the turquoise robes as I tie the mask around my face. It covers the top of my forehead and eyes on both sides, then sweeps over to the left, where it curves around towards my chin in a kind of tear-drop shape.

8

MIRA

The next morning, I wake up with a thrill of excitement after my dream of the Mysteries… There was something so magical about it.

After a few moments of lying in bed, playing over the dream in my head, I get a message from Gino to come to his place to talk to him. My only other plan today is to eat and binge read so I decide to get the conversation with Gino out of the way first. He did not look happy when he discovered I'm still married, so I figure it might be a tense conversation.

I get to the big high-security steel door that leads to Gino HQ and press the buzzer. The door opens almost straight away and I head down the hallway sneaking glimpses into the rooms containing servers and multiple computer screens on my way to the red door of Gino's apartment. This is where he runs his ethical tech company, Mercury Inc, from... although what that actually involves, I have absolutely no idea.

I push open the door to Gino's modern apartment, so strikingly different to Theo's style that most of El Cielo has been designed in.

Gino is standing in the kitchen, he flashes me a smile and I'm glad he's not upset with me... although, come to think of it, I've never seen Gino in a bad mood, he's almost ethereal – the way he seems to float over the mundane concerns of daily life with his wit and his charm and his devilish good looks that seem to belong more in a fashion magazine than reality. Gino's smile is warm, but he doesn't approach me. I notice his hands are busy with the espresso machine. Their quick movements remind me of the night we danced in the rain and then made love, while he spoke Italian to me... or the super-hot threesome we had with Elias... I'm lost in my sexy memories when Gino speaks.

"Coffee?" he asks.

"Yes, please," I say, despite the fact that I've already had one back in my rooms and having too much caffeine gives me the jitters.

I wander out to the balcony while Gino makes coffee, and look out over the grounds of El Cielo. I know Elias' cottage is somewhere over to the side, beyond the vegetable gardens, and that Helio's hut it somewhere in the forest, but I can't quite see either of them. I can, however, see a glimpse of the El Cielo lake where, not so long ago, Helio fucked my brains out. The thought sends a shiver of desire and a pang of longing through me... *is it really possible... can I have them all?*

"Penny for your thoughts?" Gino says.

I blush, not quite ready to share that particular thought with him.

"Just... just thinking about how much I love it here," I say to him.

Gino's face darkens, for a moment, then he shakes his head and returns to his cool neutral expression.

"What?" I ask.

"It's just... I'm still trying to work on the immigration details for you. This... revelation – about your marital status may have thrown a spanner in the works."

"Does it bother you?" I ask

"Not personally, Mira. Only in that it complicates things. You'd think the authorities would have no interest in this kind of detail, and usually they don't, but it seems Clifford Maxwell has good lawyers and they are trying to make it look like something fishy is going on here. I do wish you'd felt comfortable enough to tell me... tell us... earlier."

"Honestly, I thought you might have known," I say. "It seemed like you did some digging into my past – you knew about me before we actually met, didn't you?"

The thought had troubled me in the past, but now it seemed so inconsequential.

"I never did," Gino says. "I saw you on the street in New York one day, and followed you, sure, but I respected your privacy. Why do you think I didn't know about the connection with Clifford Maxwell?"

"I don't know," I say, shrugging. It's kind of nice to know that Gino wasn't snooping on me, but it doesn't really help my current predicament.

"I don't want to have to leave here," I say. "Ever…."

Gino smiles at me. He takes my hand and brings it to his lips. "It's good to hear you say that, *cara mia*. We wouldn't want to be without you… not after how long it took to find you in this lifetime."

"That's the other thing I keep thinking about," I say. "The mystery of this place - of why we are all here together again – you all talk about wanting to get it right this time, but I don't even know the rules of the game… maybe none of us do."

"Please, just tell me what you know," I say. I can't help the feeling that Gino is hiding things from me.

"Your guess is as good as mine, Mira. I've been trying to figure it out – trying to solve the mystery… for years. I'm hoping, now that you are finally here with us, we will unravel the reason behind it all."

"You said you had something to tell me, Gino," I remember. "Isn't that why you invited me here?"

"Ah," Gino says. "Yes… of course." He looks a bit uncomfortable. I watch as he clears his throat and rakes a hand through his hair. "This thing – with the immigration. It might make things simpler if you leave the country for a while, and reapply for your European residency, given the way things have been held up here. There's a loophole that might work to our advantage."

"What?" I ask. My heart is racing in my chest. I never want to have to leave El Cielo, what if I'm not allowed back into Spain… what if I can't come back, and I'm stuck, far away from these men who are my soul mates?

"Relax, Mira," Gino says, squeezing my hand. "Just for a little while, just to make a new residency application. I could come with you if you like."

"You'd do that?" I ask. Gino has a way of making me feel safe and well-cared-for, without seeming to try.

"Of course, anything for you," he says, looking into my eyes. "I was actually thinking we could make it into a research trip – we could go to Greece and try to track down the temple… you know, the one from our dreams. I have some clues about where it might be."

In the space of less than a minute I've gone from feeling panicked and distraught at the thought of having to leave the country, to feeling joyfully excited. "That would be amazing!" I say. "I'm *very* interested… It would be fascinating to see a place in real life that I've only dreamed about… even if none of it is still there anymore."

"You're right," says Gino. "There might be nothing left. It could be built over with an apartment building or a mall for all we know."

I nod. "Yes, but even still, I'd want to go there… to see how it feels to be there again."

"Elias will probably want to come too… since it's a chance for him to show you his homeland," Gino says, eyeing me carefully. "I haven't asked him yet; I was waiting to see if you were interested."

The thought of having Elias and Gino to myself in some hotel suite is enough to make my mouth water… especially after the incredibly sexy night we shared just a few days ago. It was my first ever threesome, but I sure as hell hope it's not my last.

"I could ask Helio and Theo as well if you like."

"Okay," I say, wondering about the chances that either of them would join in the sexy times… Theo seems unlikely to be into it, but with Helio, it could probably go either way.

Gino has a look in his eye that tells me he must be reading my thoughts again. He looks as if he's going to devour me! *And I sure as hell wouldn't stop him…* He leans towards me, reaching out to brush a stray strand of hair away from my face.

"Mira," he says, his voice is almost a purr, and I practically melt.

A sound rings through the apartment – like an old-fashioned doorbell.

"Someone's at the door," Gino says, distracted from our intense sexy moment. *Dammit.*

Gino gets up and glances towards a panel on the wall, which I realize must show the footage of who is outside.

"It's Elias," he says. There's a tightness in his voice, an anxiousness. "But you were here first Mira, and I don't want to interrupt…"

"No," I say. "It's fine; let him in."

Maybe I can convince them they want a rematch of our threesome the other night...

Elias enters the apartment and there's a strange look in his eyes. Gino looks back at him. I see a lot of history there, and pain, and suddenly, I want to leave them alone to resolve whatever is going on between them.

Elias looks from Gino to me, suddenly realizing I'm in the room. He looks conflicted.

"I'm sorry to interrupt," Elias says. "I should go."

"No," I say. "Please don't. I was just leaving."

Knowing that they both adore me and wanting them both to get used to doing it at the same time – so I have a vested interest in them sorting out their feelings for each other. I suddenly feel brazen. I turn and kiss Gino lightly on the lips and then walk over to Elias, giving him a slightly longer, lingering kiss... after all he is officially my boyfriend. Then I step away and walk towards the door. Casting one last meaningful glance over my shoulder, I say "I hope to be seeing you both again soon..."

My words are so loaded that I don't dare stay to catch the look on their faces. I bolt down the hallway and out of Gino's place, cackling to myself in my head the whole time as I allow myself to imagine them both pleasuring me at the same time again, and an even more kinky fantasy... *pleasuring each other too... oooh... I never even knew I was into that.* I flash back to glimpses of my dream... of the Ancient Greek life... of the early morning by the river... *delicious.*

I make it back to my rooms, but I'm feeling overly aroused, and I'm craving something to take the edge off... *or someone.* I decide it's the perfect time to pay Helio another visit and take him up on his offer.

9
MIRA

I change from the simple but elegant silk tunic I was wearing for my visit to Gino into something less expensive and more durable – my jeans and a tight black top with a V-neck that shows off my cleavage. My impression is that Helio is not one to care what I'm wearing, as long as it's easily removable. He's not interested in anything pretentious; he likes things to be wild and untamed… in fact, he's not even interested in cuddles. I found that out last time we were close, or as I've come to think of it: the fuck and run incident, but maybe that's exactly what I need right now.

I don't bother with shoes, since Helio never seems to when he's running around the forest, and since I know the paths through the trees are smooth and worn, if a little gnarled with tree roots.

I head through the El Cielo buildings and outside, towards

the forest. As I walk, my hand brushes against the rough bark of tree branches. I hear the kiss of falling leaves, and notice that some are turning golden and orange. When I arrived just a few weeks ago, the forest was lush and green, and now I'm seeing the seasons change, and I want to be here for them all. I'm afraid to leave... to miss anything... but most of all, I'm terrified of the possibility that I might never be able to return.

I take the path that I think leads to Helio's place, enjoying the smell of trees and fresh damp earth from the gentle rain last night. I spot mushrooms and toadstools as I walk, releasing their own musky scent. The forest is beautiful, but for some reason I can't seem to find Helio's house.

The track I take leads me in a circle, and so I take a different one. I end up at the lake. I take a moment to enjoy its still, glassy surface, reflecting the clear sky and autumnal trees.

Didn't Helio lead me through a forest path from here directly to his house? I look in the direction that I think is the right one, and see what looks like a narrow winding path. I figure I'll try my luck. *It's not like the forest here is big enough to properly get lost in...*

Half an hour later I've lost all sense of direction. *Boy, was I wrong...* I've somehow managed to get lost in the El Cielo forest, and I don't know which way to go next. Part of me knows that it's fine – that I'm safe – that everything will be okay... but there's another part of me that's getting more and more panicked, and it's the part with the overactive imagination... *What if Victor has been released from custody and he's after me; he's out here, waiting to get revenge on me for ruining his life... What if Cliff is out here with another one of his surprises?*

Of course, I'm more likely to be attacked by someone else out here: a stranger, a wanderer with a violent past, an opportunist kidnapper... but those realizations don't make me feel any better.

The panic builds up in my chest. I hear a thump... *It could be a fallen branch, or a footstep!* I need to protect myself from threats. *Maybe if I act crazy, no one will bother me...*

I start to run, screaming, waving my arms in the air.

It's actually kind of fun and I'm pretty sure no one will be brave enough to attack me now. The path in front of me widens, and then suddenly, I glimpse him: a man is running towards me! I can barely see him through the strands of my dark hair flying wild in front of my face – it's too late to stop or run away, and I crash straight into him. His arms wrap around me and I can't escape, and for a moment, the panic intensifies to a fever pitch, then the man speaks my name and I realize I've run into the very man I was looking for in the first place.

"Helio?"

As my heartbeat slows to normal, it dawns on me that Helio is standing here in front of me, wearing only a pair of black shorts and a light blue denim shirt that's undone, revealing his entire chest and tight abs... *mmmm.*

"Mira – what the hell were you doing out here? I thought you were being attacked."

"Uhh..." I say, standing back and brushing the hair out of

my face. "I was... I was actually coming to find you," I admit, blushing. "But it turns out, I don't know the way to your place. I thought it would be easy to find by myself, but I got lost in the forest... and then..."

"And then you decided to scream and wave your arms around to ward off bears?" Helio says, laughing.

"Not bears..." I say.

"Good, because there are no bears here," he says. "But you were scared?"

There's a rare note of concern in Helio's voice as he looks at me with those dark eyes. I notice that his long wavy hair is pulled into a topknot, and I want to untie it, to set it free, to feel it brush against my naked skin...

"Mira?"

"Oh, sorry," I say. "I got distracted."

Helio smirks. "Oh yeah?"

"But..." I say, recovering my focus. "I guess I just got scared of being attacked by someone... you know... after Victor."

Helio wraps his arms around me, protectively. Knowing how un-cuddly he normally is, the gesture brings tears to my eyes.

"You've been through so much," he says. "Come, I'll make you a hot chocolate."

"Really?" I say, taken aback that wild, stoic Helio would make such a thing.

"You know... it's a Spanish tradition," Helio says.

"Of course," I say, recalling that the Spanish were, in fact, the first people to invent sweet hot chocolate drinks after they'd been pilfering it from South America and their queen or princess or something decided she liked to drink hers with sugar.

Helio takes my hand and leads me through the woods. It's a nice feeling, being guided by this big, strong, hunky man. After a few moments, his cabin appears, and I feel foolish for not just walking slightly further along the path I was clearly already on to find it like a normal person!

It surprised me, at first, to find that Helio didn't live in the main buildings of El Cielo like Theo and Gino, and that he had built himself this very rustic shack out here in the forest, but that was before I knew him better. Now it makes perfect sense. Helio thrives in nature, in the wild. He might be a well-regarded engineer, but he would probably be quite happy living by himself in the wilderness out of sight of civilization.

Helio opens the door to his cabin and leads me inside. The warmth from his wood-burner is a welcome change from the chill of fall, outside. He pulls up a chair for me at the small wooden table and I take a seat as he turns back to the kitchen. He takes a cast iron saucepan from its hook on the wall.

I enjoy watching him as he begins to add ingredients: water, cocoa, spices, honey, to the saucepan… he places the saucepan on top of the wood-fired stove to heat, and brings the hot cocoa drink to a simmer. Then, he reaches into a cupboard, which I quickly realize is a refrigerator, and retrieves a bottle of cream, which he adds to the mixture.

"I didn't realize you have electricity out here," I say as Helio pours the delicious smelling concoction into two brown pottery mugs.

He shrugs. "Solar panels on the roof," he says, passing me a mug.

I smile and take a sip of the thick, warm, spicy drink. It's exactly what I need. I can feel my body responding, relaxing, unfurling like a tight bud finally letting go of its fear, and blooming towards the sun.

"You were coming to find me. What were you after?" Helio asks, looking at me.

I blush again.

"Another booty-call?" Helio says, laughing again.

"Maybe," I say, grinning sheepishly.

Helio puts on a mock-offended look. "I'm more than a piece of ass, you know, Mira?"

"I know that… but you're also a great piece of ass," I say. I'm not quite sure what I'm going for with that statement, it comes out kind of muddled, but Helio is non-plussed.

"As are you, Princess," he says, returning the somewhat strained compliment with the pet name I kind of hate, although the more I get to know Helio the more I don't mind being his princess.

I blush. "Uhh… Is that okay? I mean… you did kind of offer…"

Helio laughs. "Hmm, let me think," He says, putting down his mug, and taking a step towards me. "A beautiful woman wants to have her sexual needs fulfilled and goes out of her way to seek me out for the task…"

He reaches for me, tilting my face towards, him, wrapping his other hand around behind my neck.

Helio's face spreads into a big smile. "Yes… I think that's okay," he says, swooping in to kiss me. He tastes of chocolate, and spices, and the wild…

Shivers run through my body. I lean back, taking a breath, and quickly put my cup down behind Helio before I accidentally spill hot chocolate everywhere. Then, I let myself melt into him, my body softening against his firmness, my lips parting for his tongue, taking it inside my mouth, wanting more.

I feel dampness build between my thighs, as Helio's hands creep down to circle and cup my breasts, rough and determined and instinctual.

He pushes my V-neck down and frees my right breast. Then he takes my nipple into his mouth, circling it with his tongue, grazing it with his cheek while his hands search over my body, discovering me, claiming me, stroking all the way down from my collar bone to my thighs, priming me for what's to come.

I'm ready. I'm beyond ready. I want to rip both of our clothes off, I want to be taken, filled, fucked… but I let my pleasure build, I let Helio take the lead… *for now.*

I watch him, looking up at me, gauging my pleasure as his hands and tongue seek out my other breast, my other nipple. Both my tits are out, hanging over my tight black top. I can see Helio's giant erection through the small pair of shorts he's wearing. I reach out and run my hands over his pecs and down his abs...

His skin feels so good, so hot. I grab hold of his shirt and pull him back up towards me, devouring his delicious mouth as my hands seek out his cock through the fabric of his shorts.

Helio groans and his fingers rub up the inner seam of my jeans, causing me to groan with him. He presses into my pussy through the thick denim and I feel like I'm already close to the edge.

His fingers find the buttons of my jeans. He quickly undoes them and reaches inside to stroke my wet, swollen pussy.

Ohhh... yes...

I hitch down the waistband of his shorts, freeing his gorgeous, engorged, pierced cock. I pump it with my hand, knowing exactly where I want it to go.

Helio lifts me, effortlessly, as if I'm practically weightless. He sweeps one arm under my thighs and supports my back with the other, and then he carries me, opening the doors, outside, to the deck where he usually likes to sleep, and places me down on the futon mattress.

The cool air is refreshing compared to the heat from the fire and hot chocolate.

Helio whips off my jeans and panties, and I pull off my own top and bra, eager to get to the naked part. Then, I reach for him, pushing his shirt down off his shoulders and casting it aside, before nudging his shorts the rest of the way off.

Helio is a sight to behold – glorious, naked, huge, pierced... and right now, he's all mine.

He lunges into me, knowing I'm ready for him, knowing exactly what I'm wanting. He spreads my legs and presses himself down onto me. His naked skin feels amazing. He kisses my throat and, and then he pauses, just for a brief moment, his giant cock nudging against my opening.

"Would you beg me for this?" Helio asks.

"Yes," I say.

"What would you do… for this?" he asks, nudging just a little bit further.

I groan. "Right now, I'd do just about anything," I say.

"What do you want, Mira?" he asks, clearly enjoying teasing me.

"I want you to fuck me… right now!" I say, reaching for his ass cheeks with both hands, giving them a hard squeeze and shunting his big rock-solid cock into me.

Ooohhh.

I should probably be smarter than this… I realize. I should probably have a conversation with Helio about protection, but my sensible thoughts are swept away in the heat of the moment.

I groan in pleasure, feeling the sensation of his cock piercing gliding on down, stimulating the pleasure nerves inside me… taking him in, all the way in… to where there's a tightness that gives way to a deep delicious pain under the pressure of him.

Fuck… me.

He feels amazing inside me, skin on skin, and by the cocky look on his face, he fucking knows it. Then, there's a change in his expression, a thirst in his eyes, and he's looking at me like I'm an oasis in a desert and he's about to drink deep.

His face plunges into mine, and he kisses me, feverously, and more intimately than ever before. I'm already so close to the edge from Helio's magic tongue. I surrender to his thrusts, and he takes me deeper and deeper into my own pleasure. The sheer size of him as he bucks his way deeper inside me filling me to bursting, and the pressure of each thrust jolts pain through me, which blends with the pleasure of my arousal and obliterates all other worries from my mind… All other thoughts disappear.

There is only here and now, only Helio… and me… only sensation. His cock plunges into me over and over, bringing me right to the edge of my own senses, then sending me catapulting out into the universe.

I'm multi-orgasmic, rolling in cascading waves of blissful pleasure that ripple through my entire body as Helio continues fucking me inside out… for what feels like hours. His stamina is extraordinary. I'm lost and floating in timeless space, drunk on my own orgasms as Helio continues to pleasure me with his cock, thrusting, rutting, panting… breathless. Then finally, he groans, his cock throbs inside me… and he collapses on top of me.

"Fuck," he says, sounding satisfied.

"Yeah…" I respond.

And then his voice changes. "Fuck, we didn't use protection."

THE SIGHT OF SEA AND SPIRIT

"Oh…" I say. "Yeah, we probably should have talked about that earlier."

"Fuck, fuck, fuck… I'm sorry, Mira," he says, pulling out and stretching out beside me, reaching for a towel that hangs on the banister of his deck and passing it to me to mop up his mess.

"I'm on contraception," I tell him, rolling onto my belly, and propping myself up onto my elbows.

"Thank the fucking gods," Helio says, and then he looks at me again.

I raise my eyebrows. "Are you…"

Helio cracks a smile. "Don't worry, I'm clean – no STDs here."

There's a wave of relief, and then a different concern presses through my mind, making me frown.

"Really, Mira, don't worry." Helio says, noticing the expression on my face. "I've been tested since the last time I was with anyone else. You can trust me."

"It's not that," I say. "I do trust you at your word."

"Then we're okay." Helio says, as if it's as simple as that. I wish it were. But I can't shake the thought of Helio fucking other girls while fucking me. He might be clean now… but what kind of risks would that open up in the future if he makes a habit of rising bareback. It takes me a minute to find the right words.

"Okay, but the thing is," I say, "…usually I wouldn't have unprotected sex unless…" I stop before I say the "R" word. I don't want to freak Helio out at the mention of commitment.

Helio's expression is curious, as if he knows he's being asked something, but he's not sure exactly what. Then after a moment, he figures it out, "I'm not exactly relationship material, Mira," Helio says. "And... the others..."

"I mean..." I say, nudging him in the shoulder with my index finger. "...If we're going to be having unprotected sex – then it's not safe for me if you're having it with other random people, too."

Helio nods. "But you'll be with the others – with Gino and Theo and Elias."

I blush. "I don't know," I say. Even though, I do kind of know... at least with some of them.

"Yes, you do, you greedy girl," Helio says, tickling me softly with his big hands, and sending more waves of desire shooting through me.

"I mean... I want to... and Elias... he's kind of agreed to be..."

"To be in a relationship with you?"

"Yes," I say. "It's all a bit weird, isn't it?"

Helio shrugs. "It's like it always has been with us," he says. "Or, maybe that's not quite right... It's fair to say that it seems this is how it always *should* have been, in those past lives – we were all drawn to you – bound to you at a deeper level, but we never quite got it right. Our egos got in the way..."

"Yeah, I know," I say. "Theo..."

"Not just Theo," Helio says. "We all fucked it up – you saw the French life in your regression. We had another chance, but all of us were too arrogant that time – too wrapped up in ourselves…"

"So, what are you saying, Helio?" I ask, and a tension creeps into my voice. "What does this mean for us now? You say you're not relationship material… you act all arrogant and then apologize and tell me you're working on it…"

"It's true," Helio says. "I'm not… and, I am… I can't give you what you need, Mira. I'm not the cuddly type. I'm not into emotional stuff."

I feel disappointed at Helio's confession. I was hoping that his feelings for me… the ones I can tell he has… would change everything. I ponder this for a moment, and then I just let go of wanting him to be anything other than who he is.

"I can accept you as you are," I tell him. "Wherever you are in your process, in your life. I mean… as long as you keep working on not being a complete asshole."

Helio laughs and gives me a playful shrug.

"Deal," he says.

"I can get my emotional needs met myself," I say. "I'm pretty self-reliant… and also, there are the others…"

"That's what I was secretly hoping," Helio says, and there's a tone of amusement in his voice. "The others can pick up the emotional labor and the mushy stuff. I'll be here to give you gratuitous sexual pleasure on tap."

"That sounds like a pretty sweet deal," I say, laughing. It's true, too… it sounds too good to be true, that he's fine about me being with the others and also having Helio here to fuck my brains out whenever I'm feeling the itch. "But…"

"You want to know whether I'm going to be seeing anyone else on the side?" Helio asks.

I nod.

"I'm not interested in anyone else, Mira." He says, and there's an earnest note in his voice – one that I rarely hear from him. "Sure, I've fucked around before – the ladies obviously go wild for me," he says, flexing his biceps. I giggle. "But honestly, it meant nothing, and you… you…"

He can't quite say it, but I can feel it *…you mean everything.*

Instead of uttering the words, Helio climbs back on top of me. "…you look like you could do with another round," he says.

After another thoroughly satisfying fucking session, I feel raw on the inside and also deeply content. Helio and I lie together, spent and exhausted, on his futon and watch the sunset. We are not exactly cuddling, but he seems happy enough for me to lean against him and look out at the darkening horizon and the sky, blooming in peachy tones in the impossibly fluffy clouds.

"Hungry?" Helio asks, and I realize I'm famished.

"Definitely," I say. "That was quite the workout."

Helio grins at me and then disappears into the kitchen. I'm curious about what he's planning to feed me. I've seen several new sides of Helio today, and I like them… a lot. He might still be the most emotionally unavailable and arrogant guy around, without even Theo's excuse of feeling emotionally tortured by his own guilt and excessive need to take responsibility for everything.

Helio, in comparison, is about as carefree as they come, but I can tell this is all part of his mask too – keeping him safe from his own emotions... *eww, emotions... who has time for those?* Well, I do, and it turns out I have a lot of time for Helio, and not just the kind of time that's permeated with, *err... good exercise... and orgasms...*

It was sweet of him to bring me here and make me delicious, spicy hot chocolate, especially given the state that I was in when he found me in the forest. He *did* take care of me... and then he *took care* of me, good and proper.

I almost wish I'd had time to finish that delicious hot chocolate though before being swept up in his pheromones for... hours. *How can it be that the sun is setting when it was only just late morning on my way out to the forest?*

I know exactly where the time went and it was worth every blissful, orgasmic second. I'm still feeling high as a kite, and obviously, my inner monologue is showing that... my thoughts are rambling *all... over... the... place...*

I hear a sound and turn back towards the inside of the cabin to see Helio emerging holding two pottery bowls in a similar style to his mugs.

"Whatever that is, it smells delicious," I say. "Don't tell me you made this?"

"This is the kind of thing I eat," Helio says, shrugging. "It's nothing special."

Helio smiles and then ducks back inside again, returning with our mugs of spiced cocoa, which are piping hot again. He's also holding a rustic looking loaf of bread.

"It seems pretty special to me! What is this?" I ask, peering into the bowl Helio passes me.

"Venison stew," he says, grinning. "I like to hunt for my food, and then I swap some of the meat for vegetables and flour and spices from Elias."

"You swap it?" I ask, giggling.

Helio shrugs. "In a matter of speaking."

He rips off a piece of bread and dips it the stew gravy from his bowl. I follow suit. The stew is delicious – it's rich and flavorful, and spicy with hints of red wine and cinnamon.

"My god, this is good," I say, prompting a smug smile from Helio.

"That's a great compliment, coming from a professional chef," Helio says.

"Don't tell me you baked the bread too," I say. It does taste homemade, a flavorful sourdough. "Or do you trade and barter for that too?"

"I make bread when I can be bothered," Helio says, casually.

"But how?" I ask. "You have no oven."

"There's a brick and clay oven around the side there," he gestures to the left of the cabin. "I fire it up once a week or so – it makes great pizza, too."

"I bet it does," I say, impressed. I take another bite and wash it down with the hot chocolate.

"Would you appreciate some wine?" Helio asks.

"Yes," I say. "But if you tell me you made it yourself by stomping on the grapes, I'm going to be proposing, forth-with."

Helio laughs. His laughter is deep, rich, and playful. It mingles with the sounds of the encroaching night around us, the final calls of the day birds, the wakening nocturnal creatures, the chirping crickets.

"No, but I do help Elias out with the wine making, so you'll have to propose to him as well," he says. "Plus – you shouldn't be joking about a new marriage, seeing as you're still a married woman."

"Don't remind me," I say, punching him lightly in the shoulder as retribution for teasing me as the dread from my predicament floods back in.

"Hey – I don't make the rules," Helio says, dodging away from me. He ducks back inside and returns with a bottle of wine and two glass tumblers. "Last year's vintage," he says.

"Wow – real El Cielo wine," I say. "I'm surprised I've never seen a bottle of this before."

"Hah – you can blame Elias for that, too," Helio says. "He likes to make it and then give most of it away to the neighboring farms and their workers. He hardly keeps any for himself or for El Cielo. He's too generous for his own good, that man."

I nod, believing every word.

Helio pours out the red wine into the tumblers and passes one to me. I take a sip. It's delicious, tangy, with notes of sour cherry and tamarillo.

"Still, you're quite the master of self-sufficiency out here," I say to Helio. "It's kind of awesome."

"Only 'kind of' awesome?" He asks, and I can tell he wants to tickle me again.

I shiver, suddenly feeling the deepening chill of the night and realizing I'm still naked. Helio notices. He disappears back inside again and returns with a big, soft angora blanket. It's gorgeous and silky and finely spun.

"This is nice," I say, putting my empty bowl down and wrapping myself up in the blanket. "I didn't expect you to have something like this."

"Hah, what did you expect?" Helio asks. "That I'd sleep under animal hide?"

"Well do you?" I say, laughing.

"Actually, sometimes," Helio admits, joining in with my laughter. "It gets cold out here in the winter. I have a good supply of different blankets and things inside."

"I can understand why you'd sleep out here," I say, taking another sip of my wine and looking up at the stars that are just starting to peak through. The light teal horizon fades to dark blue above us. I lie back on the futon and Helio joins me, his body giving off enough heat to power a small town. I hardly need a blanket with him here to lean on.

"Please tell me you make your own cheese too?" I say. "I've always dreamed of having a… lover…" I choose my words carefully, so as not to make him retreat. "… who can make his own cheese."

"I may have dabbled in a few batches of manchego," Helio says casually. "But you'll want to go to Elias for cheeses as a general rule. He's really your dream man; I'm just the cherry on top."

I giggle, and relax under the stars. My body is responding again to being in such close proximity with the very hot and very naked Helio, but I'm a bit too sore to act on my desire.

"What do you think it all means?" I ask Helio, trying to distract myself from the renewed throbbing desire in my pussy that's wanting more despite being rubbed raw already. "All this past lives stuff. You talk about getting it right this time between the five of us, but why... Why is any of this happening?"

"Ahh, the great mystery," Helio says. "Gino knows more, have you asked him?"

"Yes," I say. "He didn't tell me anything. It felt like he was holding something back."

Helio shrugs, not filling me in on whatever it is that he knows Gino knows. "I won't pretend I haven't thought about it... I want to know as much as any of us do, but maybe that is just beyond our comprehensions in our mortal forms."

I laugh, *Mortal forms. You make it sound like we're supernatural beings who have come to earth just for the sex,"* Helio raises his eyebrows again.

"That must be it," he says, reaching for me again.

I lean back, away from him, turning my head back up towards the sky.

"Too much sex for your poor little body to handle?" Helio asks, his words are joking, but his voice sounds concerned.

"Something like that," I say. "Don't get me wrong. It was amazing, I just feel… a little tender inside."

"I have an idea of something that might fix that," Helio says. he leans into me, running his hands down my body, parting my legs, stroking me softly, gently in a way that surprises me.

My previous sexual encounters with Helio have all been rough and fast, but now he moves, smoothly, subtly, masterfully, like an experienced craftsman. He shuffles himself down the futon until his face is right up against my pussy, and then he licks me, slowly, and tenderly like an ice-cream cone, pausing to gently suck on my clitoris, artfully applying pressure there, until I'm a puddle of goo, putty in his hands, as he works me, effortlessly, closer to the edge of orgasm. Shivers run through me, right across my skin, to the tips of my fingers and toes… and then Helio hums into me, catapulting me into another out-of-body-experience. I'm seeing stars, not just above me, but all around me. I am stars. I'm floating.

"My gods, you are delicious," Helio says, watching me as I continue to come, and I don't think he just means the taste of my pussy, though by the way he's licking his lips, that might be part of it.

Helio collapsed back onto the futon, in a satisfied sigh.

"This is the life…"

I lie there, next to Helio, enjoying the heat of his body, savoring this rare moment of intimacy with him, where he's relaxed, and he seems to have let go any pretense of putting distance between us. I'd return the favor and suck his cock, but I am all floppy; I can barely move.

"Can I sleep here?" I ask.

He raises his eyebrows at me.

"Just tonight, I mean."

"You can sleep wherever you want, Mira," Helio says. It feels as if he's brushing me off, becoming distant again.

"Don't do that," I say. "I'm not asking you to be my emotional-support-pony, I just don't want to move right now… or for the foreseeable future."

Helio laughs, and warmth returns to his voice. "Sure, you can sleep here. Just don't expect me to get all cuddly or anything."

"Fine," I say. "No cuddles are required. But I may need to requisition your bodily warmth to be my own personal furnace."

"That settles it, then," Helio says. "Sign me up for hot-water-bottle duties," and despite his insistence that he's not the cuddly type, Helio puts his arm around me, and pulls me close, breathing me in deeply, into what might look and feel exactly like a cuddle, but clearly, is definitely, absolutely not a cuddle at all.

I smile to myself, snuggling into Helio's warmth, and gently drift to sleep.

10
MYA

It is the night of the Mysteries, I'm with the other priestesses. We have dressed in the robes we drew out of the sack offered to us by the High Priestess Alessia.

"When we wear masks, we embody the gods and goddesses," Alessia says, putting on her mask, resplendent in light green and golden hues to match her robes. "Tonight, I am Persephone!"

We all break into applause, as if a pantomime has begun, calling out and stamping our feet. The excitement is so palpable now, as if I could reach out and touch it.

We, the uninitiated – those priestesses who have not taken part in the Mysteries before – are led to a small chamber at the back of the hall. We sit in the dark while the eunuchs play soothing music outside. One by one, we are blindfolded and led away.

When it is my turn, the blindfold is placed over my mask. Soft hands reach for mine, leading me out of the chamber. I can see down, through the bottom of my mask as we walk across the stone floor.

I am led to the altar. I hear Amedes' voice. "Do you, priestess, in the form of Artemis, lay down your pride and mortal desires to surrender to the will of the gods for this initiation?"

"I do."

I am led in a circle around the altar. As those surrounding me chant the names of the gods and goddesses, I feel drops of water sprinkled onto my skin and smell incense unlike any I've known before. I return to the foot of the altar.

"Are you ready to let go of this mortal attachment and surrender to your fate?"

Am I? I wonder. What am I getting myself into?

There seems to be no other option at this point, and I'm comforted to know that this is Amedes speaking, even if he's Amedes embodied by a god. I think back to the ritual just a few weeks before on this very altar – Amedes as the god thrusting himself into me. I shiver.

"I do."

I hear the sound of liquid being poured into a vessel. A chalice is lifted to my lips and I drink, deeply... it tastes of the earth, of the sea, of the rivers... it tastes of bitter herbs, and memories, and regret, and forgiveness, and the pleasure-pain of lovemaking. It's so delicious, I want to drink more, and yet, it's almost unbearable in its complexity.

When the chalice is emptied, the blindfold is removed and I can see through the eye holes in my mask. I stand before Amedes and Alessia, and the other priests and priestesses.

"Welcome, initiate Mya!" Alessia says, embracing me. Her full lips briefly press against mine, along with the soft exposed skin of her *upper-chest, neck, and shoulders. Next, Amedes embraces me. I enjoy the feeling of him – his hot, firm skin and muscle, pressing against me. I'm embraced by all the initiated priestesses and priests in turn. Then we turn to the next uninitiated priestess.*

When we are all initiated, we leave the inner sanctum of the temple, walking in procession into the outer reaches to the sound of the pan pipes played by the eunuchs. At sunset, the gates to the temple compound were closed to stop any late arrivals from interrupting the ceremony.

From behind the pillars, I can see that a small crowd has gathered within the compound, waiting to be initiated into the Mysteries too. They are all wearing masks and have brought blindfolds with them as instructed. These people are from the village and beyond. Any free person can be initiated into the Mysteries, or so I've been told by the other priestesses.

I catch a glimpse of a familiar, tall, well-built man, and something inside me sings out for him. I know it's him – the blacksmith, Teris, and I can't stop myself from wanting him. As our eyes meet, there's a jolt of energy between us – despite our masks, I can tell there is a connection.

One by one, we lead the waiting crowd through to the temple. Those who have already been initiated may pass through and wait in the main chamber, those who haven't are led through to be initiated in much the same way I was. When it is Teris' turn, I make sure I am the one to approach him. I take his blindfold and reach up, to wrap it around his mask. I lay my hand on his forearm, and tingles rush through me.

"Have you been initiated into the Mysteries before?" I ask him.

"No," he says, his voice quavering slightly.

"Come with me."

I lead him confidently, as if I am the expert even though I'm actually only slightly more experienced in this than he is. As we walk, warmth spreads through me that is not at all related to his body heat.

As I lead Teris towards his initiation, warmth continues to spread out from his touch, setting me aflame. I feel a tightness in my forehead and a slight queasiness, and I wonder if these are related to the gorgeous man I'm guiding or to the Mysteries themselves. I know so little about what is to unfold.

I watch as Teris is initiated and then embraced by each priest and priestess in turn. I am last to embrace him, and as the others are preoccupied with the start of the next initiation, I let my hands linger just a little bit longer on his arms and lean in, inhaling his musky scent.

My body longs for him, to pull him closer... for him to dive into me and satisfy all my urges, but I hold back, knowing both our lives are at stake. I remove Teris' blindfold and allow myself one more long gaze into those deep, dark eyes filled with just as much longing as I feel. He looks back at me, as if hypnotized.

"Welcome, initiate," I say, smiling at him.

I lead Teris back over to the other initiates, and return to the ceremony. Although my thoughts are full of the handsome blacksmith, another initiate catches my eye. He moves with an elegance and swiftness that seems familiar.

It's hard to tell who he is under his bright blue mask, and matching robes. I appreciate the way the fabric drapes over his lean *musculature. I watch him through the initiation process, wondering what's so familiar about this man. It's not until we embrace at the end of the initiation that I recognize those familiar arms around me.*

"Alfio," I whisper, so that only he can hear me. "I didn't think you'd be here."

"I wouldn't miss it for the world," Alfio whispers back, squeezing me gently.

I take his arm and lead him to sit near the other initiates, watching Teris' eyes on me the whole time. As we walk, shivers seem to dance between us.

Maybe this is the Mysteries potion taking effect.

As I turn back towards the others, I walk straight into another initiate. His blindfold has already been removed, and the green eyes that show through his mask are familiar.

I feel another wave of delicious desire.

What is going on with me? Why am I suddenly falling all over all these men?

But even as I thought that, I realize it's only very particular men who capture my attention – no others have caught even the slightest bit of my interest. There's something special about these ones, and even though I barely know them, I can feel the palpable connection between us.

It's going to be an interesting night.

11
MIRA

The sound of morning birdcalls wake me up. I open my eyes to bright sunlight. I realize I had another dream about the Mysteries, as if that night is more prominent somehow than all the other nights of the temple life.

It used to be that I dreamed of past lives nearly every night, but I haven't had quite so many lately... not only that, but somehow, I'm outside. It takes me a moment to remember why, and another moment to realize I'm alone. Helio has gone. I suppose expecting him to stick around for morning definitely-not-cuddles was a bit too much to hope for.

I lie there, on the futon, thinking about the dream... thinking about Teris... who is now Helio, and how different he is now compared to then. His soul is the same, but the energies of his body in this life make him different, wilder.

I sigh, wrapping the angora blanket around me to keep warm against the cold morning air. I drift in and out of sleep again, half expecting, half hoping that Helio will come back and *entertain* me some more even though I'm still sore from yesterday's antics. I wait here for a while, but he doesn't show. He's probably hiding from some newly realized vulnerability that he's not quite ready to face yet. The thought makes me sad.

In the spirit of accepting Helio as he is, I decide to leave him alone to deal with things in whatever way he seems fitting, so eventually, I summon the willpower to get up and get dressed. I contemplate taking the blanket with me because I'm still freezing in just my top and jeans. It would also be an excuse to visit Helio later, or to get him to come and visit me, but in the end, I decide to be a big girl. I shrug it off and leave it on the futon. I find a scrap of blank paper and a pen inside the hut and scrawl a note on it for Helio.

Thanks for the delicious evening. I'm still sore, but I'll be up for another booty-call whenever you're ready for me.

I hope the note strikes the right balance of casual and sexy, rather than sounding desperate or needy, or angry, even though I might feel a tad of that from waking up alone after the exquisite night we just shared… *never mind…*

I leave my note on the table, but on my way out, I discover another note pinned to the back of the door. It's a hastily scrawled map of the El Cielo grounds. With the three main features being "Helio's sex shack," which is, I assume, where I'm standing now, "Mira's not-princess palace", and "sexy lake."

THE SIGHT OF SEA AND SPIRIT

I giggle to myself, and take the note. It warms my heart somewhat, to know that Helio has gone to the effort to help me get back. Not only that, but on the back, there are a couple of messy scrawled lines.

"To help you find your way next time you want some satisfaction."

Mmmm...

I smile as I make my way back, through the forest path in the direction of the main buildings of El Cielo. Despite the fact that I'm using a hastily scrawled map, it's actually quite accurate. As I walk, I wonder what other parts of the El Cielo grounds I could christen with hot Helio sex – that might eventually make it onto the map. A fantasy plays in my mind of finding him fixing the water pump again – sweat glistening on his chest as he works in the hot sun – him taking me, right then and there, up against the tank, or on the ground in a patch of soft grass... *Mmmm...*

Mira... what the hell has gotten into you? I ask myself. *It's like the switch has been turned on and you're suddenly a nymphomaniac.*

I guess there's something about sexual energy that feeds on itself, igniting my latent desires ...that spreads like wildfire. I wonder if that is how I can get all four of my guys into bed with me at the same time... *just keep turning up the heat with them until they can't control themselves.*

I wish that I'd brought up the group sex thing with Helio, because after my experience with Gino and Elias, and after all the sexy dreams I've been having, I can't get the thought of it out of my head. I'm curious to know how adventurous Helio really is under all that bravado, or whether the cock-piercing is just for show.

12

MIRA

I arrive back at my rooms to find a brown paper bag sitting on the floor outside my door. My heart races.

Not another gift from Cliff!?

For a moment, I panic, and then, I realize Cliff would never use any kind of packaging as humble and unassuming as this. There's a note on top.

I thought it was about time you read this.
Love, Gino, XX.

There's a book inside. I glance at it, figuring it's another volume on reincarnation, which I don't think I really need since I'm quite clearly convinced it's real by now.

I take a long, hot shower as soon as I'm inside. I get almost too hot in more ways than one, thinking about Helio and fantasizing about the other guys …all at once. I'm so aroused that even after I flick the shower dial over to cold to try to cool off, I'm still flustered when I come out.

How is it possible to still be aroused after all the sex I've had?

I guess it's just like I thought – *sexual desire begets more and more of itself unless it's distracted or diverted somehow.*

I can't seem to distract myself now, so instead, I get into bed and find a raunchy group-sex scene in the reverse harem novel I've been reading, and then I imagine my guys in place of the guys in the book.

Despite still feeling raw, I stroke myself gently, imagining Gino going down on me, while Theo binds my hands to the bed with silk ties, then undoes his fly and thrusts his cock into my palm telling me to stroke him.

I imagine Helio with a cocky smirk, offering himself into my other hand, while Elias pleasures Gino with his mouth and strokes my body with his hands. I'm close to the edge already, and then I imagine Theo switching places with Elias, so he can fuck me, while Helio claims my mouth and cups my breasts…. And it's all too much.

I come, breathless and panting, into my pillow, wondering if the real thing could work quite as smoothly as my fantasies.

13
MIRA

I lie in bed for a while, enjoying my self-created post-orgasmic bliss. I don't have any work to do today, but there's a lunch function tomorrow. Life is just so much cruisier here than it ever was in New York. I finish the novel I was reading and then I decide to pick up the book from Gino, figuring I might as well do some more research. It's called *Life between Lives*, and I instantly find it enthralling.

It's written by a guy called Dr Michael Newton, who started off as an atheist who didn't believe in anything silly and spiritual like reincarnation. I can instantly relate as I had similar beliefs only a few weeks ago. He was a professional counsellor with a PhD, and was quite well-respected in his field. He was using hypnotherapy to help patients recover from trauma, and then one day, he accidentally regressed someone back, not just to an earlier point in their childhood, but much further back.

I've heard of cases like that before. There are other books on Theo's bookshelf with similar stories of regular hypnotherapy somehow turning into a past life regression, but this one goes much, much deeper.

Dr Newton at first thought people were just inventing these "past lives" and wanted to test his theory, so he experimented, and his curiosity led him to finding a whole deeper level of hypnosis where his clients spoke about not only going between lives, but about what happens in between, about going home to the spirit world.

"Where are you?" Dr Newton asks one client.

"Here in my permanent home," comes the reply.

Tingles run down my spine as I read this. Something in this concept is resonating with me deeply – so deeply that I feel like I intuitively understand it more than Dr Newton seems to. *Of course... this world... this physical form we are in here on Earth isn't really home... It's like Gino said to me once – we are here to learn. We come here to this world, which is like a kind of multi-dimensional learning environment, and when we leave our lives... we go HOME.*

Suddenly everything is making so much more sense. I'm struck by awe at the realization, which is followed by frustration with Gino. He clearly knew all about this. *Why didn't he tell me or give me this book earlier?*

I push away my frustration and focus on the new information instead. I still don't know why we've come here to this particular life, but I know where we've come from... at least, I'm starting to, and that's another part of the puzzle that I was missing.

When people leave their physical bodies, after death, they are reunited with their "soul group" a group of special souls that they share a deep connection with – that they share many lives with.

Is that what we are? ... a soul group? Does that explain why we keep reincarnating together across multiple lives?

Something rings true about this and I'm pissed off that Gino never told me about all this. *It makes so much sense.*

This is big... this is exactly what I've been wondering about... what I've been asking all the guys about. *Why the hell didn't they tell me?*

Time for a group meeting... I decide. I text all the guys and tell them I want to meet with them all. *We have important business to discuss,* I write in the message. *Unless anyone else has any objections, let's meet at 6pm in Theo's office.*

Then I put down my phone and go back to the book.

I'm struck by what one of Dr Newton's regressed clients said to him while in deep hypnosis *"I miss some friends in my group and that's why I get so lonely here"*

It hits me that my whole life, up until very recently, was permeated by a feeling of loneliness. I was missing my soul group – these wonderful, infuriating, sexy-as-fuck guys, and now that I've found them, that's all changed. I knew my life was different here, but it never occurred to me before now that the biggest change has been internal. *I'm not perpetually lonely anymore.* I used to be lonely, and I used to fill the void with cheap margarita mix, trashy movies, and pizza… Now, I feel connected. I've found my soul group. *They are my home…*

The spirit world as the book portrays it based on multiple examples is captivating. The clients in hypnosis describes travelling through a tunnel of light. One of them describes entering the spirit world like travelling through layers of a cake. It's all so surreal, and yet on some level, this book resonates with me – deeply and profoundly, like nothing I've ever read before.

I still can't believe the guys never told me about this. Surely they've all read it, or at least know about it. Surely, Gino would have shouted about it from the rooftops when he discovered it… come to think of it, I remember seeing Dr Newton's books on Theo's shelves, and yet, despite me continually asking them questions about the purpose of all of this – of us all coming together in our lives. For some reason, none of the guys mentioned to me before that there's a whole book – practically a guidebook, mapping out how and why we come into our lives and where we come from, and return to in between lives.

I knew there was something they were holding back… The fact that they were hiding something so significant from me after all we've been through – it really grinds my gears!

14
MIRA

By the time six pm rolls around, I'm furious. I've been pacing back and forth in my room, rehearsing the kind of things I want to say to the guys – of course, I need to ask them why they didn't tell me about this – why they skipped over these highly important details.

I've even put on the sexiest dress in my wardrobe – for effect – because I want to make them pay attention to me, and because it's an excuse to try to turn up the heat and spread a little more of that fiery sexual desire around to see what catches flame.

The dress is floor-length, black silk, with a long slit right up to the thigh and thin spaghetti straps that crisscross at the back. I've paired it with my reddest lippy, and an extra coat of black mascara. I've curled my hair so that perfect ringlets flow freely down my back, instead of the usual messy waves.

I wait until a few minutes past six because I want to make an entrance. I'm sick of not being told the full truth. I'm sick of being patronized and treated like a child. I'm going to show the guys who's boss.

I open the door to Theo's office and strut in. The room is large, with Spanish gothic windows, and walls of bookshelves. At one end is Theo's desk and on the other side is a suite of green velvet sofas where the guys are waiting for me.

It's satisfying to see the expressions on their faces. Their jaws drop when they see how I'm dressed. I pace across the room a few times for good measure. Then I stand in front of them with my hands on my hips – clearly this is not usual Mira behavior. They all look surprised, confused, and hungry for me.

Good... that's the exact effect I wanted to have.

Finally, Theo asks, "What is it, Mira? Why did you call us here?"

It must be slightly odd for Theo to be summoned to his own study, but that's not really a concern for me at the moment.

"I wanted to talk to you all about this book," I say, pulling it out of the black tote bag I brought with me.

"You called an urgent meeting to talk about a book?" Helio asks, amusement plays on his lips.

"Yes," I say. "Exactly... because I started reading this book and realized it had all these answers in it that no one had thought to inform me of before. So, I'm asking, did you all know about life between lives? And if so, why the hell didn't you tell me before?"

Gino looks uncomfortable, he clears his throat, and then says "Apologies, Mira. I didn't give you that book earlier because I didn't want to overwhelm you."

"Overwhelm me?" I say. "I'm not a child, Gino, and I'm sick of being treated like one. I've been asking questions about why we are all here – together – since I first found out you all had the dreams too, that it was some kind of reincarnation thing. Now I find out you knew a lot more, and you just weren't letting on."

"It's just a book, Mira," Theo says. "Just one theory among many."

"It's not just a book," I argue, struggling to find the right words to explain how profoundly this particular book is affecting me – how much it resonates, making me tingle in recognition.

"You're right," Gino says. "It's not *just* a book or a theory... That particular book is significant. At least, it is for me. That's why I lent it to you. I thought you were ready."

"And you didn't think I was ready before?" I ask.

Gino lowers his gaze.

"I see... and I suppose all of you have read this book?" I look to Elias and Helio. They both nod.

"A long time ago," Elias says. "But I recall it had a profound effect on me. I don't think it's just a theory, either. It's well-researched, but more than that. It rings true."

How is it that Elias manages to put into words everything that

I'm thinking and feeling, far better than I can? There's sadness in his eyes as he speaks and I guess he's upset for me – that I got frustrated enough to call a meeting over this.

"The thing is," I say. "I feel like this is important – this book in particular: soul groups, and the reasons why souls come into physical lives… Reading it makes a whole lot of other things make sense… and the fact that no one mentioned it before, or recommended it, or lent it to me… It feels like you've all been keeping secrets from me – drip-feeding me information. And that also makes me wonder what else you're holding back from me."

"Are you serious?" Helio says, and there's something in his tone that makes me freeze. "You accuse us of keepings secrets from you – you didn't even tell us you were married!"

The accusation feels like a slap to the face. "So, it did bother you!" I say.

Helio looks away from me. "I didn't say that," he replies. "It's just that you're making a big deal about this… It shows you have trust issues…"

"Excuse me?" I say. I didn't mean for this to turn into an argument, but I guess it has. I feel frustrated and stressed and furious with the lot of them.

"We're sorry, Mira," Elias says. "We really are. We didn't do anything with the intention of hurting you. Please believe me…"

I sigh. "I do… I guess. It's just… so frustrating."

"This is what secrets do," Helio says. "On both sides. You keep things from us to protect us or protect yourself… We might have been slow to tell you things. Maybe… maybe we should have told you everything to begin with, but then I'm sure you would have run a mile. The problem is, the things we do to protect each other – they are the same things that often come back to hurt us… all of us."

I'm stunned by Helio's profound words. I can tell that me keeping my marriage from the guys did affect him too… even if I never meant to hurt any of them.

I let out a long slow breath.

"I'm sorry," I say. "I guess I was in denial about being married to Cliff… maybe I'm still in denial about a lot of things. It's really hard, even the thought of him…"

Tears are running down my cheeks, messing up my mascara, but I don't care. I'm flooded with a wave of emotion, so deep and old and painful that I don't have the energy to care. I fall to my knees and sob as the flashbacks pour into my mind. The memories of extreme powerlessness – of being locked in the cupboard by my father, locked in the apartment by Cliff… threatened with violence by both of them.

"What is it?" Theo says. "What's wrong?"

"It's a trauma response," Elias says. "Just give her some space, talk gently to her… Mira, we're here for you; you're safe now… okay… Everything is fine now. It's okay… just relax."

I curl up into a ball. Elias' words are like a cool balm to my inflamed emotions. I can sense him slowly moving closer to me; then he gently strokes my back.

It's starting to dawn on me that I might have been overreacting... I mean all they did was not happen to mention a book to me... *why is that so triggering?*

Calling this meeting and confronting all the guys now suddenly feels out-of-proportion and foolish. The shame hits me hard and I sob again.

"There, there," Elias says. "You're safe now; you're with us, and we love you. We will protect you."

"We have to get that man – Clifford Maxwell – out of her life," I hear Theo say to the others. There are murmurs of agreement. "I've made some inquiries," Theo continues. I prop myself up on the floor, wiping the mascara tears from my eyes, and look at him.

"What kind of inquiries?" I ask.

"This might not be the best time..." Theo says.

"No, tell me. Please?" I ask. "I can't bear to have any more secrets. Please tell me everything."

"Very well," Theo says. "I've inquired about divorce. It should be easy in Spain – quick and painless – once you're formally a resident, that is... as we have no-fault divorces here."

"Okay, thank you," I say, comforted that Theo has figured this out.

"In that case," Gino says. "We should leave the country as soon as possible. We go to Greece for our research trip and apply for your residency. You'll be able to get the divorce as soon as we're back."

"How soon are you talking?" Helio asks.

"We could leave tomorrow," Gino says.

Everything feels so rushed, all of a sudden. "Tomorrow is too soon… isn't it?" I ask.

"Or next week," Gino suggests.

"I'm coming with you," Elias says. "If you'll let me be your sexy Greek tour guide."

I laugh. "Of course."

"Who else wants to come?" Gino asks.

"I'm up for anything," Helio says, winking at me.

"Of course, you are…" I reply.

"I'd better stay here," Theo says. "Take care of business…"

I feel disappointed that Theo doesn't want to come on our adventure, but I'm excited that the others do. Then it strikes me that rushing off to Greece in order to get the residency and get the divorce is not going to solve all my problems.

"I don't know whether this will work," I say. "I do want a divorce… like I said. But I don't think it will be that simple getting Cliff out of my life for good."

"What do you mean, Mira?" Theo asks

"Cliff is repeating lives with us too – remember? He was in the French life and I have a feeling he was in the Ancient Greek life. Remember Pellis? The General who killed us all? I'm sure that must have been Cliff. The profile fits. It might well be his fault we keep dying before we do whatever it is we come to do here… I just figure if this is a multi-lives thing, divorce is probably not going to cut it."

"You're probably right," Elias says. "We need to tread carefully. It seems like this guy has a history of reckless and violent behavior. But we need to get you residency, anyway, if it's what you want."

"What is it that you want, Mira?" Elias asks.

"I want..." I look around at all the gorgeous guys that I'm starting to fall in love with. I know I probably look like a wreck right now, but it's about time I brought my feelings out into the open. "I do want residency, I want to live here, but... no more secrets between us, right?"

There are murmurs of agreement around the room.

"Then I'd better tell you that what I want is to be with you – all of you," I say, looking at each of the guys in turn, noting the expressions dawning on their faces, interest, curiosity, confusion.

"You've been with all of us," Theo says, crossing his arms.

"I want it to be official," I say. "I want to be in relationships with all of you. Like you all keep saying this is 'meant to be'... we're meant to be together. I want to get it right this time, and... If you want to know what I really want... I want to be *with* all of you... at the same time."

Helio gives me a cocky smile and then cracks into an expression of mock-outrage. Elias and Gino seem less surprised by this announcement, but they both look across to Theo who has a furious look on his face. He stands up and storms out of his own office.

The four of us are left behind in silence.

"Just being honest..." I say, and the others laugh. I join in the laughter, but it's a bit strained. None of us want to hurt Theo, and yet... he's left me alone with three incredibly hot guys who basically just told me they were up for group sex.

I think back to my threesome with Elias and Gino, and feel an extra thrill at the thought of Helio joining us.

It's tough being torn between guilt and arousal. The distressed look on Theo's face makes me want to go after him, to see how I can make things better…

After a few moments, my conscience gets the better of me. "I better go and check on Theo," I say. "But I'm not going to forget what you guys just signed up to… I'll hold you to it."

"Wait, Mira," Gino says, and I'm half hoping he's about to coax me into sexy times right here and now.

"What?"

"Are you okay for me to plan our trip for a few days' time?"

"Sure," I say. "Book a big hotel suite too," I wink at him and walk towards the door.

"Ah, Mira?" Helio says, and the sound of his voice really makes me wish I could just have them all now, but Theo's study is hardly the right place…

"What, Helio?" I ask, trying to sound sultry.

"You might want to wash your face first – I mean, I might like it when you're a hot mess, but I think Theo has more refined tastes."

I blush and laugh and then leave the room, giggling to myself on the way.

It's probably just as well Helio reminded me, because when I look in the mirror, my face is all smeared with mascara. I don't know about hot, but I certainly look like a mess.

I wash my face, but I don't bother getting changed. Then I go upstairs to Theo's apartment.

I knock on the door, but there's no answer. Theo is doing the aloof thing again, but I'm not having any of it.

"Theo, I know you're in there," I say.

Still no answer, so I turn the door knob, relieved to find it unlocked.

"Theo," I say. "Don't ignore me, please."

Theo looks out the windows. He turns towards me as I enter.

"Not now, Mira," Theo says, turning his back on me again.

I take the opportunity when his back is turned to slip off my dress and panties, and take off my bra. I let my clothes fall to the floor.

Try ignoring me now.

"Theo?"

"I said not now," Theo says, glancing back in my direction. He freezes at the sight of me, stark naked in his room. A look comes over him: pure desire.

"Lie down on the bed," he commands. His voice is a low, delicious growl. "Now! ...and choose your safe word."

I do as he says, throw myself down on my front, on his bed.

"What's your safe word?" Theo asks. "Tell me."

"El Cielo," I say because it's the first thing that comes to mind and because it makes me feel safe. With my head turned to the side I catch a glimpse of Theo's face as a big smile spreads across it. He steps closer to me and I feel my pussy clench in anticipation as a jolt runs through my body.

THE SIGHT OF SEA AND SPIRIT

"Are you feeling safe?" Theo's voice is a horse whisper in my ear, and it's sexy as fuck, but still I double check.

"Yes." I trust Theo, and I know he only wants to give me what I need.

"Have you been a bad girl, Mira? Do you need to be punished?"

I never thought I'd be into this kind of talk, but it's really turning me on.

"Yes," Theo slaps me hard on the ass, and I like it. Moisture builds between my legs.

"Imagine we are back at the temple," Theo says, his voice a low, gravelly whisper. "You've been a very bad priestess. Haven't you?"

"Yes, my priest," I say. The memories of Theo as Amedes flood back, along with the atmosphere of the temple that night... the tension building as he laid me down on that altar...

"I might have to tie you up to punish you, don't you think?"

"Yes," I say, my body tingling in anticipation as I catch a glimpse of the black silk scarves as he begins to tie my hands to the bed posts with them.

Theo gets down close to my face and whispers in a low voice that makes my entire body quiver. "I've caught you with the others, and now you need to do your penance, to offer up your body to the God."

"I submit to your will, my priest," I say.

This is sexy as fuck and I'm loving it. I feel an aching need in me, and want Theo to fuck me right now, but I can see he's enjoying it too much, and so am I.

"I remember…" Theo continues, "…how sweet and innocent and virginal you were, my Mya."

My mind flies back to the temple dreams, to the night Amedes first made love to me.

"I do…"

"The other priestesses were chanting all around us, blindfolded, as I, your high priest… I led you up to the altar that night… Do you remember..?"

"Yes," I say.

Theo crouches down beside me, his voice becoming so deep and low it makes me melt.

"I took the form of the God and claimed you on the altar… you offered yourself up to me… you embodied the Goddess… my goddess… my conquest… You liked that, didn't you?"

"Yes."

He smacks me again. My body quivers in response. I relax further into the bed, almost as if I'm dissolving – as if I'm surrendering a deep anxiety, a deep terror that I've been carrying around all my life. I'm safe here with Theo, and he's more than willing to discipline my old fears away.

"You liked that, didn't you?" Theo says in his deep velvety voice, "You bad, bad girl… You liked how they were all there, surrounding us as we fucked at the temple."

"Yes."

Theo slaps me again with his open palm. The pain burns deep into me, transforming into a kind of jagged pleasure that I never even knew existed.

I melt deeper into a puddle on the bed as Theo runs his

finger up my inner thigh, into my wetness. He whistles, taking in the state of me, and how ready I am for him.

He lingers there for a moment, making me want him, making me wait. Then, he lifts his hand and sucks my juices off his finger.

"It turns you on when I slap your ass, doesn't it?"

"Yes."

Theo whacks me again, sending a tingle right to my clit.

Holy shit...

"You want me to fuck you now, don't you, Mira?"

"Yes!" I moan into the pillowy surface of the bed, gripping the silk ties with my hands, writhing into the duvet with intense desire.

Theo's hand comes down hard against my ass, sending another jolt of pleasure and pain through me and making me beg for him.

"Please," I say. "Please...please fuck me now."

"Patience, Mira," Theo says. He steps away from the bed and comes back holding something. I only get a glimpse of it, but it looks kind of like... *a feather duster?!*

Something cool and soft brushes against the back of my legs, right up to my thighs, sending shivers through me... *oh my gods...*

"Do you like this, Mira?" Theo asks. "Do you like the caress of feathers?"

"It feels... amazing," I say.

"Good," Theo says, teasing me with the delicate softness. Even though it feels lovely, I'm craving something much, much harder inside. I moan as my desire rumbles through me, like a deep cavern needing to be filled.

"Please... please, Theo..."

"Please what?" Theo asks.

"Please, fuck me... hard."

There's so much tension in the air, so much naked desire and wanting in my voice that even Theo in all his stoicism can't resist. I can hear the sound of his belt being undone, his fly unzipping, a condom packet tearing, and then he's behind me on the bed, tilting my hips up, seeking out my entrance with his fingertips, sighing when he feels how I've become even more wet from all his teasing and slapping.

He enters me hard and fast from behind. I groan as his cock hits my g-spot, filling me perfectly. I'm still tender from Helio fucking my brains out last night and that makes this even better, somehow, as if I need the pain... as if I need to go deeper into it, and into myself, in order to heal.

Theo's hands search up between my skin and the bed, until they seek out my breasts, cupping them and using the purchase to thrust again and again and again. The friction and force Theo creates is grinding my clit into the bed over and over.

"Do you like to be punished, Mira?"

Theo whispers into my ear as his stubble grazes my neck.

"When it's by you, I do," I say.

Theo slaps my thigh and I groan breathlessly into the bed. Then, he thrusts again, biting down hard on my neck. The sensation is so intense, so much pleasure and pain, that it rocks me right to the edge. There's an implosion inside me as pain and pleasure collide... emotion comes flowing out – all the darkness, old trauma, fear, pain and despair is releasing somehow... it's rushing forward, through me.

Holy fuck.

Then Theo intensifies the pressure, clamping his body down over me, tightly. I can feel his breathing on my neck, giving me goosebumps as he takes me deeper into myself than I've ever been. His hard, sharp thrusts are so deliberate, and lingering, teasing out the pain they are drawing from deep within...

Then, as I cry out in pleasure from the intensity of it all, Theo builds momentum with his thrusts, like an engine picking up steam, gaining speed and force... sending me right over the edge into a spectacular orgasm, and out floating into space.

15
MIRA

The next couple of days are filled with getting ready for the trip to Greece. There's a sense of excitement in the air that reminds me of Christmas when I was a very young child, when my mother would be decorating the house, putting up the tree, making me a special cup of cocoa every night, and letting me open one of the bright colored windows or doors in my advent calendar, revealing a sweet surprise behind each one.

Of course, now my sweet surprises are all related to the sexy Mediterranean men I seem to be well on the way to falling in love with. Although I hardly see Theo, who has retreated into his shell again since our last intense encounter, I spend a lot of time with the others, plotting and planning, and flirting.

Elias has been showing me parts of Greece on a well-worn

paper map, and describing things about the climate and local foods. His enthusiasm is always so infectious. Hearing him speak about his homeland makes me want to visit every single part of it, taste every local dish.

We've agreed to fly to Athens and then go to the place Gino thinks is the old site of our temple – all those hundreds… thousands of years ago. After that, we're going to visit the Greek island that Elias grew up on. I wonder if we'll meet his family, and if he wants to introduce me as his girlfriend. I don't mind. I hope the others don't either.

I pack my suitcase, taking mostly my own clothes and a few of the things Theo bought me. It feels strange to take the expensive items out of my wardrobe and put them in my luggage to be crumpled with everything else, especially since Theo won't be around to enjoy them. *That's his choice,* I tell myself, but it still troubles me that Theo is always so hard to read. I never know where I am with him. I wish he would suck up his jealousy and come with us.

"Will it be busy?" I ask the guys. It's the morning before our flight and we're having a shared breakfast in the dining room, made by Calista, so of course it's full of delicious pastries. I take another *pain au chocolat* because I can't help it – they're so good.

"It's not peak season," Gino says.

"Yes," Elias agrees. "As it's autumn now, it will be less busy than July. Fewer tourists on the beaches."

"How did you work out the location?" Helio asks Gino through a mouthful of croissant.

"It's a ten-day journey from Athens on foot – that's what I remember from my dreams, so I mapped out all the places that it could be, and studied the satellite imagery. It needed to be by a river of course."

Of course. My mind flicks back to the raunchy past life dream of all four of us at the river… The guys around me must be thinking the same thing, and they blush slightly, except for Helio, who just has a cocky smirk on his face. I don't think I've ever seen him blush.

We all meet in the lobby with our luggage. Helio just has a small satchel slung over one shoulder, and Elias has a backpack, while Gino has a leather carry bag and two elegant looking suitcases, that look like they are from some elite Italian designer.

I smile at how different my guys are. They are pretty much dressed to match their suitcases too. Gino is in an expensive but casual shirt, with a brown Italian leather jacket over it. He's wearing dark grey trousers, and shoes that match his jacket and look like they cost more than what I earn.

Helio is wearing a singlet and shorts, with a worn dark blue jacket slung over his shoulders, and hiking boots, and Elias is in a clean white linen shirt with dark blue jeans. They all look so good that I can't help having naughty thoughts. *I can't wait to get them out of those clothes.*

The guys had argued, yesterday, over whether to order a driver to get to the airport, but in the end, Helio won with his bid to drive us all in his big car. Once we're all assembled, Helio takes off in a run to get it. A couple of minutes later we hear a low rumble and turn to see an absolute beast of a vehicle pull up outside the front of the lobby. It looks like a shiny black military truck, with all those square angles, but I still intend to tease him about being a soccer mom with a people mover.

We all climb in. Elias offers me the front seat, but I insist he takes it instead, and I jump in the back with Gino who casually rests his hand on my knee, sending waves of pleasure and anticipation up my thigh. I want him to move it up, higher, inch, by inch. I want him to fuck me in the back of the car while the others watch in the rear-view mirror, stroking themselves through their pants until they can't bear it any longer and they are forced to pull over to the side of the road and join in the back-seat shenanigans.

"Mira?" Gino says. "Are you okay? You have a strange expression on your face."

I blush.

"Just thinking about our trip," I say, leaning into Gino and inhaling his expensive cologne.

I didn't think it was possible for my mind to get any dirtier, but here we are. I restrain myself and tease Helio about being a soccer-mom instead, and I can tell he thoroughly enjoys it. Aside from the teasing, I'm on my best behavior the entire car-ride, despite desperately wanting to rip Gino's clothes off.

As we pull up to the Barcelona airport, a heaviness comes over me, a sadness that Theo isn't here with us. There's a deep longing I feel for him now, especially after the night we just shared. I wish we could all go on this trip together – to *be* together. I can't bear the thought of being separated from Theo – or from any of my guys. I have the urge to call him – to beg him to come – to delay our flight just for him, but I know he will refuse. I've never met such a stubborn bastard in all my life.

As we get out of Helio's car in the airport parking, I can't hide the sadness from my face. "What is it, *latria mu?*" Elias says. "Are you unhappy to be going on this trip? What do you need?"

"Oh," I say, wiping away a stray tear that I hadn't even been aware of. "No, I'm excited about the trip it's just…"

"Theo," Gino says… in his uncanny way of reading my mind.

"Yes."

"He'll still be here when we get back," Helio says, walking over and wrapping his big muscly arms around me. "In the meantime, you'll have to make do with the three of us." He cocks his eyebrow suggestively, sending a jolt of sexual electricity right to my pussy. I practically have to lean against him to stay balanced.

Is this really happening? Are we really about to embark on a four-way sexual adventure… in Greece?!

I have no idea how my life got to be this good. As I walk with the guys, towards the airport, my sadness about leaving Theo behind evaporates in the excitement of what's to come.

I start to head in the direction of the main counters, but Gino pulls me aside.

"Oh, yeah," I say. "Tickets?"

"We don't need tickets where we're going, Mira," Gino says.

"What do you mean?" I ask. "It's an airport. We're going to Greece. Surely, we need a plane ticket."

Gino smiles. "Follow me," he says, leading us in a different direction. We reach a small counter off to the side. Gino rings the bell, and a beautiful dark-haired woman appears dressed in a tight black jumpsuit, holding a clipboard.

"Inara!" Gino says, kissing her on both cheeks.

I can't help but feel a pang of jealousy.

"Lovely to see you, Gino," the woman, Inara, says. Then she greets and kisses the other guys. She pauses when she gets to me. "Who do we have here?"

"This is Mira," Gino says.

Inara raises an eyebrow, but doesn't say anything. She smiles at me and kisses me on both cheeks as well. I'm quite confused by this stage.

What kind of airline are we flying on? One with sexy jumpsuits as a uniform and super friendly flight attendants?

"Let's go," Inara says, leading us down a passageway and out onto the airport runway.

"What…" I start to say, and then Gino finally explains.

"We're taking my company plane. I thought it would give us more privacy."

It's my turn to raise my eyebrows.

Gino laughs and says, "not for *that* reason, Mira. I meant because of Clifford Maxwell's stalkerish behavior. I wouldn't want you to be stuck on a plane that he, or any of his henchmen, are on. It might not be safe."

"But Cliff owns part of your company," I say. "Surely, this isn't safe either."

"He's just a silent partner," Gino says. "And hopefully not for much longer, but either way, he has nothing to do with the running of the company."

We board the small, elegant plane. I feel like a movie star. Of course, the seats are all like comfy couches and booths, and they're all covered in El Cielo's signature green velvet. The walls are paneled with a light wooden veneer. The whole place looks and smells expensive.

"It's like a freaking hotel, isn't it?" Helio says.

"Isn't your company supposed to be ethical?" I ask Gino, taking a seat on one of the velvet sofas, which is just as comfy and luxurious as it looks. "What's with all the carbon miles from private air travel?"

"Sometimes it's a necessity," Gino says, sitting next to me and putting an arm around my shoulder. His hand rests against the top of my breast, sending shivers through me. "But don't worry, we carbon offset – so this flight will plant hundreds of trees, alone."

Helio laughs and mutters something about green capitalism.

I ignore him and smile back at Gino. I notice we are alone, just the four of us... of course there's a pilot somewhere up in the front cabin, but there's a solid wall giving us some semblance of privacy.

"Ever joined the mile-high club, Mira?" Helio asks, clearly thinking the same thing.

THE SIGHT OF SEA AND SPIRIT

I shake my head.

"This might be your lucky day..." Helio's words send another jolt of desire through me, but I take one look at Elias and I can tell he's not in the mood.

"Are you okay?" I ask.

"I'm not so good on airplanes," Elias says, looking pale. He's almost green during take-off, but seems to calm down, and then falls asleep.

The rest of the flight is surprisingly peaceful, even though I might have been happy to have a bit more action.

It only takes about three hours to fly to Athens, which Gino insists is the best airport option for security reasons. I wonder what kind of security arrangements he's actually been making behind the scenes.

What does he know that I don't about Cliff and the risks my ex-husband poses?

The plane swoops down. It turns and circles over the striking blue of the Aegean Sea against the jutting base of the southern peninsulas of the Greek mainland. We circle back and then rise higher over the hills to land.

I stare out of the window at the sea and the thousands of small white and grey buildings that make up the city spread below, beneath the steep mountain range. It's hard to imagine, this is the same country where we once all lived, many hundreds of years before. The modern industrial activity evidenced below feels wrong to me, in a way that's almost painful. I want the Greek world of my dreams – of my ancient life where there were only buildings of stone and mud and clay, and forests, and fields tended by hand. This looks like a different place, like an industrial desert compared to the lush climate I remember.

"It's the farming," Helio says, noting the look on my face and pressing his forehead against the plane window next to me. "It happens everywhere that people live for a long time. They farm all the productive capacity out of the land, leaving it dry and prone to erosion… and these days they build factories as well which adds to the pollution."

I sometimes forget this side of Helio – the side that's not only a professional engineer, but also an ecological designer whose vision lead to El Cielo being the lush micro-climate that it is today, unlike the dry fields and vineyards of the surrounding area. I wrap my arms around him and lean into his delicious muscular torso.

"Better put your seatbelt on, Mira," Helio whispers into my neck. "We're in for a rough ride ahead."

An announcement comes over the plane intercom. It's a woman's voice telling us to take a seat and put our seatbelts on. It sounds kind of familiar, and I wonder why there was no such announcement on take-off when Gino had simply told us what to do.

The questions circling in my head are quickly forgotten as the plane lurches to an abrupt landing on the runway.

I look at Gino and he shrugs, then heads over to open the door, letting in a flood of warm Mediterranean air through the air-conditioned cabin, and suddenly, it feels like I'm coming home all over again. It's a strange sensation, and I almost want to cry. I felt similar on arrival at El Cielo for the first time… similar, but different.

We leave through the airport and get into the car waiting for us on the other side that Gino has organized.

Helio has a grim expression on his face as we drive through the city.

"No trees," he says through gritted teeth. "I hate cities, especially when there are hardly any trees like this. At least, Barcelona has trees all through it."

"Hah," Elias says. "You're not wrong there, my friend. There's a reason people call this city "cementopolis." There are far fewer trees in Athens than most places."

"Can't we get out of here?" Helio says to Gino.

"We're planning to stay here just for the night, remember? Tomorrow we set out for the other side of the peninsula. That's where I think the temple site is. There will be trees along the way, don't worry."

"Can't you even handle one night here?" Elias jokes. "So much for being a big tough guy!"

Helio looks livid.

"It's okay, Helio," I say. "I don't mind changing plans if it puts you at ease."

"No. It's fine," Helio says. "I can handle it, just don't expect me to be perky."

"We don't usually," Gino says with a laugh. "I've come to expect many things from you, Helio, but "perky" is not a word I'd use…"

"Yeah, yeah…" Helio says, still sounding grumpy.

16
MIRA

After a brief stop at the embassy to get the paperwork started, we arrive at the hotel, which is sleek, and modern, and very Gino. We check our bags in at the front desk, but we don't even make it to our suite before Elias excitedly drags us off to roam the streets of Athens. Being back in his home country has brought a new liveliness and confidence to Elias that I haven't seen in him before, outside of our more... intimate... moments, anyway.

There is a beauty and a charm to Athens, and also a roughness that is different from the refinement of Barcelona. Helio was right, there are hardly any trees, but many of the streets are cobbled. There are too many buildings that look like they were designed and built in the 60s in that particularly ugly era of architecture, and that makes me sad, thinking of all the older buildings and ruins that must have been demolished in

THE SIGHT OF SEA AND SPIRIT

the name of progress... but the streets we walk through this sunny afternoon are lively – filled with brass bands playing and street vendors with stalls selling delicious looking things like olives, pistachios, dried apricots, and fresh produce. There are markets filled with antiques and clothing, and some very unusual looking guards standing stock-still, wearing little red tasseled caps, pleated black kilts and white stockings.

"It's something to do with celebrating the end of the 400-year occupation of the Ottoman Empire," Elias says.

"Do they just stand there all day?" I ask.

"Yes," Elias replies. "It's like the English who have those guards with funny hats outside the Queen's house. At some point they march around and then get replaced by other guards."

"Ridiculous," Helio says.

The guard in front of us maintains his neutral expression.

"You Spaniards can talk," Elias retorts. "Your traditional guards look like they're about to strip for a hen's night."

"But look – the giant pom poms on their shoes!" Helio crows. "How is that supposed to look threatening to anybody?"

The guard's face reddens slightly.

"You know, those pompoms traditionally have concealed knives inside of them," Elias says. "For sneak attacks... you better watch out, maybe they still do."

I giggle at Elias' explanation while the guard looks Helio in the eyes prompting him to gulp. It all seems so surreal. The Ottoman Empire took control of Greece for 400 years, and yet centuries before that, we were here, or somewhere near here, living out our lives. A shiver runs through me at the thought.

We continue our walk, and I look up at the hills rising above Athens and at the Acropolis, which seems to perpetually be looking down over the city.

"It was once a strategic point," Elias says, pointing up towards the pillars that still stand of the Parthenon. "And it was considered an entrance to sacred parts of the city."

"What does Acropolis mean?" I ask.

Elias shrugs, "It just means the highest point of a city."

"You'll find the Greeks are a very literal people," Gino says, jabbing Elias playfully in the shoulder. Elias smiles and reaches for Gino's hand. An intimate look passes between them that causes tingles to run through me. *I've got to get them into bed together... with me...* I blush, thinking back to our threesome. *How much hotter would it be if Elias and Gino were pleasuring each other at the same time as they pleasured me?*

"When are we heading back to the hotel?" I ask. "I'm getting a bit tired."

"Soon," Elias says, putting his arm around me and looking at me tenderly. "But first, I must feed you."

The sun is just starting to set and Elias leads us past a range of casual looking dining establishments. "This one is my favorite," Elias says, leading us into a big cozy taverna filled with round tables covered in white tablecloths.

"Lucky we are so early," Elias says, "Because it gets packed out by 10pm."

"Isn't 10 a bit late for dinner?" I ask.

Elias raises his arms palms up into a shrug. "Not in Greece," he says.

We are seated at one of the larger round tables. Elias orders two carafes of the house wine despite Gino's obvious distaste, and then goes wild on the menu, ordering just about everything for us all to taste.

"Oh… you'll have to try their dolmas, Mira," he says, adding yet another thing to the increasingly long order, much to the waiter's amusement.

I take a sip of wine and relax back in my chair, listening as a musician starts playing a stringed instrument in the corner. I take a closer look. "Wait, is he playing some kind of banjo?"

The guys all look, then burst out laughing.

"No, that's a mandolin," Gino says.

"Actually, it's a bouzouki," Elias corrects. "It's similar to a mandolin, but more… Greek." We all laugh this time. It's nice to relax with my guys in the cozy atmosphere of the taverna, but the more I enjoy myself, the more pangs of sadness I feel at leaving Theo behind.

After my second glass of the house wine, which even Gino admits is actually pretty good, my sadness turns to anger. *How dare Theo be such an aloof sulk that he never wants to participate, that he's so emotionally unavailable he can't even be there for me when I need him...*

Then I have a flashback to our last night together and my anger turns into desire. I want him to tie me up again. My sultry thoughts are distracted by the arrival of dozens of plates of food that cover the entire table.

As we begin to fill our plates with the amazing smelling food, the man with the bouzouki starts to sings in a rich, deep voice that reminds me of Theo. Of course, I don't understand the words but the way he sings sounds beautiful and tragic.

I open my mouth to eat an olive from the roast vegetable salad in front of me and the flavor is so intense that I have to close my eyes to experience it. It's delicious, salty, tangy, and deeper and more complex than any olive I've ever eaten before. The experience is so overwhelming that I feel tingles through my whole body – a genuine food orgasm. *Oh. My. Gods....*

I open my eyes to find all three of my guys staring at me.

"It's good, no?" Elias asks.

"That was out of this world," I say.

"Are you going to try some?" He asks the others.

"I'd be quite happy to sit here and watch Mira eat olives all night," Helio says and Gino nods in agreement, his mouth still open in surprise.

Before long, we all dig in to the amazing food. We devour the succulent grilled eggplant, enormous lemon prawns, crispy roast potatoes and tender lamb set out in front of us. I've never been the biggest fan, but I even eat a couple of dolmas. I still don't really get the appeal of cold rice, even if it is wrapped in grape leaves and pickled, although these might be the nicest ones I've tried so far.

After a while, we are satisfyingly full and slightly tipsy, and the food has been polished off without any going to waste thanks to Helio's enormous eating capabilities. Elias insists we order the honeyed yogurt for dessert. Gino and I protest that we've eaten far too much already.

"You must," Elias says. "You simply must try… even just one spoonful."

We finally relent and the waiter brings out bowls of the thickest, creamiest yogurt I've ever seen, drizzled with the darkest, thickest honey… almost like a treacle.

Elias was right. I simply must devour the entire bowl, no matter how full I am. The combination of tart and sweet and creamy is all just so perfect. After a small glass of Ouzo, which is definitely growing on me, Gino informs us that the car is here to pick us up. We pile in and drive through the night-time streets of Athens, with all their clubs and restaurants and partiers and tourists out enjoying the nightlife. I couldn't be happier to be here, safe and warm, in the back of the car with my guys. I sit in the middle, between Elias and Helio, while Gino rides up front, and I can't help but wiggle a little to get closer to them both.

17
MIRA

It's not long before we are back at the hotel. We take the lift up to the top floor and open the double doors to reveal the very modern and elegant "Gino style" penthouse suite. There are four large bedrooms with king-size beds and as soon as I see them, I'm contemplating how we could push them together and create a huge bed for all of us. *Patience, Mira, I tell myself. There's no need to rush. You have the four of them to yourself for the whole trip.* Before I even have time to look around properly, Helio has stripped off naked and jumped into the hot tub in the corner of the main room.

"I thought you said this isn't really your style," I comment as I pull off my dress and follow him in wearing only my bra and panties. The wine has made me feel bold, and I feel sexy as fuck.

"Heh," Helio shrugs. "When in Rome…"

"Well, I'm glad you're in a better mood than earlier," I say as the hot water soothes and relaxes my entire body. I sigh deeply and look up to see Elias, reaching over me, passing me a glass of champagne.

It's like I've died and gone to heaven… or the spirit world, or wherever people go…

Gino has stepped out onto the balcony to make a call. I gaze out towards him as Elias hops into the hot tub in his boxer shorts. The view outside catches my eye.

"Where are you going, *latria mu?*" Elias asks as I get out of the tub, wrapping myself in a fluffy white towel. It's like the view itself is calling me. I walk out onto the balcony, as if in a daze, barely catching the words Gino is mumbling into the phone. It takes me a while to realize he's even speaking in Italian, so they aren't words I recognize.

The city lights at night are captivating, but the thing that is drawing me out here is the Acropolis. It's the view of the Parthenon, lit up at night right in front of us, high up and looking down over us the entire city. Gino hangs up the phone and comes over to stand by me.

"I chose this suite for the view," he says, wrapping his arms around me.

"It's stunning," I say. "It reminds me…"

"Of the temple… yes," Gino says. "Yes, me too. Clearly, it's not… I mean, we were in a much smaller city than Ancient Athens. We surely would have known if we were Athenians and had the patriotism to show for it."

"But the style of the Parthenon… it's so similar to the temple in my dreams."

"Yes," Gino says. "That's what makes me think it was built in a similar time."

"When?"

"Almost 2500 years ago. I'm no expert, but I have asked around, made some inquiries about other temples built around that time…"

"I'm sure you have," I say, leaning into Gino. I always appreciate how clever he is, how insightful, how gorgeous… I look into his eyes and I want nothing more than to kiss him, but the others are still inside. I glance in their direction, wondering if they would mind me kissing Gino in front of them. I expect to see them still in the tub, but to my surprise they have jumped out. Helio is sprawled on the couch, and it looks as if he's snoring.

"Shall we go back inside?" Gino asks.

I nod and follow him in to find that Helio is indeed snoring. Elias pops his head out of one of the rooms. "It's been a big day," he says. "Time for bed, I think. I'm in here if you need me," Elias says, looking at me, and not at Gino. I turn toward Gino to see disappointment in his eyes.

Whatever is going on between them… I really hope they can figure it out, and fast!

"I guess it is kind of late," I say. I take my suitcase to one of the empty rooms, ignoring Elias' open invitation on purpose. I say goodnight to Gino then take a quick shower to wash off the tired energy of the day, and the chlorine from the hot tub.

I put on a cream-colored silk negligée that I'd brought with me, thinking it would come in handy for sexy times. It doesn't look like there are going to be any of those tonight. I sigh and hop into bed. I read for a few minutes and then my eyelids feel heavy, so I switch off the light and lie in the dark for what feels like an eternity. My thoughts are circling round and round, going over everything I remember of the Ancient Greek life, going over all my hopes and fears about this trip…

I can't sleep… I finally admit it to myself about half an hour later. I wonder if I still have that sleeping pill in the bottom of my makeup bag. I get up to find it, and then I hear a noise. It sounds like a door opening. My heart races in fear, but I can't possibly go back to sleep now.

I pull a soft minky throw blanket over my shoulders and quietly open the door to my hotel room. I peek out. Everything seems to be just as I left it. Helio still snores softly on the couch. Then something catches my eye outside on the balcony. I squint out through the tinted glass to see… *Gino?*

Gino is out there again. So either, he is trying to deal with some new problem that has come up or he just can't sleep, like me. I pull the blanket more tightly around my shoulders and follow him out to the balcony again. Gino turns towards me when he hears the door open.

"Mira."

"I couldn't sleep," I say.

"It has been a big day," Gino acknowledges. "Hell, it's been a big month."

"I know. Can you believe it was only about five weeks ago that we met?" I ask him.

"No," Gino says. "...and that's because we've known each other for thousands of years."

I step towards Gino, and he wraps his arms around me again.

"What's keeping you awake?" Gino asks me.

"I'm worried about the residency thing, and I'm also worried that we won't be able to find the right place – the site of the ancient life," I tell Gino. "...That the whole trip will be a waste of everyone's time and that we won't get to stay together in the end and I will be alone... without all of you."

"Sounds like there's far too much on your mind," Gino says, sliding his hand gently down my neck to my collarbone, pausing there for a moment, before moving it lower still to caress the top of my breast through my negligee.

Mmmm... as much as I want to continue this, there's something bothering me.

"But I do have something to be worried about, don't I?" I ask him. I can see it in his eyes. He wasn't just out here enjoying the view.

"Mira..."

"Don't try to hide it, Gino. Remember, no more secrets?"

Gino sighs, letting his hand fall away from me. I'm not having any of that. I pick it up and put it right where it was before.

Gino raises his eyebrows.

"Continue," I say. "And tell me at the same time."

Gino cups my breast and, wrapping his other hand behind my waist, he draws me forward and kisses me, mesmerizing and passionate. *That's more like it.*

I pull back after a few moments and look into Gino's green eyes. They look silver in this lighting. "Now tell me, and then we can continue this."

Gino grins. "You're quite something, when you're feeling confident, *cara mia.*"

"Ummm… thank you? But I'm serious, I want to know what's troubling *you*.

"Well, first, I'd like to tell you not to worry about any of that stuff. I've done my research on the location, and even if I'm wrong, we will have more information to move forward with. And don't worry about the residency visa either. Ultimately, Mira, we will try any angle, any possibility, until we find something that works for you." He says all this while looking deeply into my eyes, and I feel moisture building between my thighs, paving the way for him to come in, but he still hasn't told me the full truth.

"So, what's bothering you?" I ask Gino. "And don't you dare take your hands off me. If it's bad, I'm going to need the comfort and the distraction and the pleasure even more."

Gino pulls me closer again, he kisses my neck and strokes my nipples through the thin silk of my negligée. This is the reason I barely need any foreplay with this guy in particular. I'm already sopping wet, just from him deftly fondling my boobs. I can't help it, I groan softly. Then he pulls back a little and looks me in the eye again.

"I got a call earlier, from our security detail. It seems Cliff has found out about our trip."

"What?" My heart races as cold terror leaps into my chest and through my veins.

"They caught a glimpse of him in Athens today near where we had dinner. It seems like too much of a coincidence…"

"Of course, it's not a coincidence," I say. "Wait, we have a security detail?"

"Yes. They are the best at what they do. You'll never notice them at work," Gino says.

My heart is facing in fear at the thought of Cliff being nearby, of stalking me, of plotting something.

"Do you want to stop?" Gino asks, raising his hand away from my breasts again.

"Hell no," I say. "Like I said, I need the distraction… more than ever."

Gino pulls me in, his hands firmer this time, and kisses me harder, more intensely, breathlessly, to the point where I can be lost in him and the rest of the world disappears.

18
HELIO

There's a moan that breaks through the cobwebs of sleep in my brain and I sit bolt-upright. *Shit. Mira's in trouble!* My heart is thudding in my chest. I look around, but the room is empty. I can't remember falling asleep on the couch, but here I am, and someone was kind enough to throw a blanket over me.

I listen closely for any sound, any clue as to which direction I should run towards to save Mira. *It's probably just a nightmare.* I tell myself. Then movement catches my eye from outside on the balcony. Someone is on the reclining outdoor lounger, but I can't quite make out their shape. There's another moan, only this time is doesn't sound like pain or fear… it sounds like pleasure. As my eyes adjust, I see them. Gino and Mira.

Mira is lying back against the cushions of the lounger,

wearing only a white slip. Her mouth is open wide, her head tipped back, while Gino's head moves between her thighs, clearly pleasuring the fuck out of her. I can only tell it's Gino because his hair is lighter than Elias, because all I can see is the back of his head.

Suddenly, I'm rock hard.

I didn't know watching someone else with Mira would do this to me. I expected jealousy, not this. I reach for myself, because I need to relieve the pressure, but it just feels too fucking creepy, jerking off, while they don't know I'm watching them.

Well, Mira keeps asking if I'm up for adventures of the group-sex kind… turns out I am.

I never bothered to put on pants after the hot tub… *prepared for anything!* I shrug off the towel that I was wrapped in, leave it on the couch and make my way quietly out to the doorway, not wanting to disturb them.

Well, shit… this is awkward… what do I say now?

I've managed to open the door so quietly that they don't even see me standing here, my cock at full attention, my piercing glinting in the moonlight. *Here goes nothing…*

"Mind if I join in?" I say, trying to keep my voice calm and casual.

"Shit!" Mira says, clearly shocked.

Gino jumps, sitting bolt upright.

And here I am in front of them both, wearing only what the gods gave me and my cock piercing.

"Well?" I ask, raising my eyebrows. "You both seemed like

you were into group sex in theory when we talked about it earlier…"

There's a moment where I realize I've made a terrible mistake. Shame prickles my skin and I wonder if I can take it back without it taxing my friendship with Gino, or whatever it is I have with Mira…

…and then something changes. There's an electric charge in the air. The tension between us is turned right up to maximum, and Mira smiles at me.

"Come on over, big boy," she says, and then covers her mouth and giggles, as if she didn't really mean to give me such a porn-star nickname. I can live with it. I've had worse, and right now, that woman could call me whatever the fuck she wants. And I'd still give her anything she asked for, especially if that thing involves my cock pleasuring the fuck out of her.

I stride towards them because the tension is pulling me closer. It's almost painful to resist.

Mira reaches for me, taking my cock in her hand and stroking it. It's my turn to moan.

Gino resumes his position with his head between her thighs. I only catch glimpses of her wet, swollen pussy. I have the urge to push Gino out of the way and claim Mira for myself, but she looks like she's enjoying herself way too much for that, and her hand on my cock is feeling really fucking good.

"I'm glad you dressed for the occasion," Mira teases me, and I want to roll her over and fuck her doggy style, but again, there's Gino, and Mira looks like she's pretty close to orgasm already. It's a blessing the gods gave women multiple orgasms. It really, really is.

I watch as Mira's other hand strokes Gino's chest and then down to his fly. She clearly wants to be getting us both off, but how can I give her more pleasure. I reach out for her, stroking her breasts and then squeezing them together firmly in the way that I know she likes. I devote all my attention to pleasuring every inch of her skin I can reach as Gino continues to eat her out.

As I circle my fingers around her nipples, she begins to shudder and a series of pleasurable moans are unleashed from her mouth as she comes. Fuck... it always feels so good to make her come, even if it's with another guy doing most of the work.

Gino pulls back for a moment, waiting for her to recover.

"What do you want, Mira?" I ask.

"I want to be fucked..." Mira practically moans, still clearly high on her own orgasm.

"Which one of us do you want to fuck you?" Gino asks.

"Both... either... I don't care," Mira says.

Gino turns to me, and raises an eyebrow.

"You first, bro," I say. "You're the one who got her into this beautiful mess..."

Never in my life did I imagine I'd be having this conversation – offering one of my best friends to go first in fucking the woman I adore... I don't even know if she'll want me after this so saying "first" is a bit presumptuous, I know, but I'm so hungry for it right now that I'm forgetting my manners.

Gino slides his pants down and his erect cock is bigger than I expected... not that I spend a lot of time thinking about my friend's cocks, and not that it's close to my enormous monster of a dick, but I admire how long his is, and that kink in the top looks as though it was practically made to hit the spot.

Mira reaches for Gino's flashy designer shirt, hungry for more. She's fumbling with the buttons as though she doesn't care if she rips the damn thing off his chest, and the sight of that sends a twinge to my cock. With Gino's shirt undone, Mira kisses him, while reaching for me again. I did not expect this to be so hot.

Gino pulls back with a determined look on his face. If I know one thing about this guy, it's that he's always wanting to make sure everyone is happy, and apparently that includes me, right now, because he pulls Mira down to the edge of the lounger so that he can position himself, on his knees in front of her, leaving her chest, and mouth, wide open for me... Mira takes the hint and reaches around behind me, grabbing me by the butt cheek and pushing me forward, towards her face. I can feel her lips kiss the tip of my cock. Just as I see, from the corner of my eye, Gino is entering her.

Fuck... me.

Mira takes me into her mouth, moaning as Gino thrusts into her. This is 500 times hotter than I expected, and we are clearly just getting started. She sucks me into her while moaning and pumping my shaft with her hand, Gino's thrusts setting the rhythm for all of us. I lean back and close my eyes, enjoying the incredible pleasure, before remembering there's more I could be doing right now... I reach out towards Mira, clawing at her skin in the way I know she likes, her groans deepen, sending vibrations right into the shaft of my cock and out into my body. *Oh... fuck...me...*

Gino looks up at us. I can tell it's turning him on, seeing me and Mira like this, and I don't even care. Surely this would turn anyone on. Gino thrusts harder, deeper into Mira. The pleasure he's clearly giving her is turning me on too, and her moaning into my cock is getting more and more intense, but something about this situation brings out my competitive streak and I want to give her even more pleasure. I hold on, drawing out my own arousal. As much as I'm enjoying Mira sucking my cock, I want to stay hard for her, to take her even further into ecstasy.

She's so beautiful as she comes... as she shivers and collapses away from my still-hard cock. A moment later, Gino takes one last deep thrust and then trembles, and comes, as he collapses forward, burying his face in her neck, just inches away from my cock.

I'm almost at the edge by now, but I want more. I want to give Mira more.

Gino pulls out and I notice he's wearing a condom, although I don't remember him putting it on. Obviously, she hasn't had "the talk" with him yet... He glances up at me, looking like he might want to sample some of this himself, but he's out of luck on that front. I don't swing that way. I only have eyes for Mira.

"Do you want more, Mira?" Gino asks.

Mira lifts her head away from my cock and looks me in the eyes.

"Yes," she says, her voice so low and sexy that I can barely contain myself. *This simply won't do.* The hardwood thing is sturdy enough, sure, but I need more room. Gino steps back as I hoist Mira up off the lounger. I kick the cushions down onto the ground and Gino grabs another one from nearby, reading my mind. He has a knack for that. As I lay Mira gently down on the cushions, she's already a messy puddle of pleasure in my hands, just waiting for more, but how to position her...?

It's "my turn" I guess, but as much as I'd like to take all of her for myself, I feel strangely as if I owe Gino some courtesy, especially since he was so willing to let me in and share Mira with me in the first place. Obviously, Mira's desires come first. I kneel beside her and stroke down her neck across her breasts to her very wet pussy. She practically purrs.

"What do you want?" I ask her.

"More," she says, grabbing me by the butt cheeks again. I growl and part her legs. She reaches up for Gino, pulling him down onto the cushions beside her. I hoist up her hips, and enter her, slowly at first. She reaches for Gino, pulling him into a kiss as he gently fondles her breasts. That's fine. I'm not here for the lovey-dovey stuff.

I thrust deeply into her, filling her, making her gasp in pleasure. One of her hands grips my shoulder, clawing into me, while the other one reaches for Gino's cock which is already hard again. *I seriously never thought I'd be into this... but hot damn.* I don't hold back. I drive my cock deeper and deeper into Mira, enjoying how tight she still is, despite her orgasm... enjoying knowing how much bigger I am compared to Gino... and how much more pleasure I can give her.

My pleasure builds as I feel hers doing the same. I groan as I feel her trembling inside, her muscles spasming in orgasm, and I know I can give her more than one...

I'm in this for the marathon, not just the sprint, and I'm barely warming up. I grab her boobs with one hand and reach around to her butt cheek with the other, intensifying her pleasure even more, as I find just the right angle to impale her.

Then I thrust into Mira again and again and again, bringing myself closer and closer to the edge. I fuck her deep and fast and hard, I let myself go like I never have before, like a raging bull, not holding anything back until Mira is screaming in pleasure and Gino's eyes are alight in awe. Then, finally, I come, sighing and trembling and collapsing into Mira.

We lie there, breathing in unison for a moment. Then there's a sound behind me and I turn.

"Elias!" Gino says.

Elias is standing there, looking out through the door at us, pain in his eyes.

Oh... shit.

19
MIRA

I see Elias at the door. The pain in his eyes is real and raw… but through the orgasmic haze it's a bit too much to deal with. Gino calls out to him, but it's too late. He's gone. I'm relieved he didn't exit through the main door, and I assume he's just disappeared back into the bedroom that he was sleeping in. Helio pulls out of me, and retrieves a towel from near the door. I have no idea how it got there, but I'm grateful for it.

It was an abrupt and unexpected ending to a magical experience, and even Helio looks somber. There's concern in Gino's eyes… he'll be worried about Elias. I consider going after him, maybe even crawling into Elias' bed, but that could be a mistake. He might not want to see me after what just happened, *and plus, I'm covered in sex juice from the other two guys.*

"Where are you going to sleep?" I ask the guys.

"I like the couch," Helio says, and I suspect it's a way for him to avoid cuddles. Clearly, he still has some intimacy issues to work through, and I don't mind giving him all the time he needs, at least for now, when I have Gino.

I follow Gino to bed and fall asleep in his arms, feeling grubby and guilty.... *but still real fucking high on sex.*

The next morning, I take a long hot shower and then throw on a linen shirt and jeans. Gino has ordered a room service breakfast of croissants and flat breads, olives and cheese. It's the kind of food Elias loves, but he doesn't seem interested. He's standing outside on the balcony, looking out at the view, or revisiting the 'scene of the crime' to torture himself further about last night... I don't know.

He turns and looks at me with that same pain I saw in his eyes last night, and it's not until later when I'm packing up that I have the realization that I wore the same outfit I'm wearing right now when we'd made love once... *was it the first time... or perhaps the last time?* I can't remember. I hope it's not actually the last time we can be together. I hope the betrayal Elias feels now doesn't come between us for good, but it's really not a good sign that he doesn't touch any of the breakfast food this morning.

It's still quite early in the morning when Gino tells us the car is here to pick us up. As we head down to the lobby, I catch sight of someone familiar, disappearing down the hallway.

"Gino," I whisper, grabbing his arm. "I'm sure I just saw that woman... what was her name? The one from the airport?"

"Inara?" Gino says. He raises his eyebrows and then shrugs. "Could be."

"What do you mean, could be?" I ask. "Don't you think it's suspicious that she's here in the hotel rather than working at the airport in Barcelona?"

I recall what Gino told me before our little adventure last night. *Cliff knows we're here, and now this woman shows up in the hotel...*

"Not really," Gino says, smiling slightly. "You know she flew us here, right?"

"She what?"

"Inara is our pilot, she flies the company plane when we need to use it."

"Oh," I say, recalling the woman's voice announcing our landing. "Okay. But why is she at this hotel?"

"It is the one favored by our company," Gino says. "She can stay wherever she wants, or course, but this is the one we recommend." He reaches out and strokes my shoulder. "Relax Mira, you are reading too much into this."

I look up to see Elias staring at us, from a few meters away. He still has that pain in his eyes, and I forget my paranoia about Cliff and transfer it to the gorgeous Greek man in front of me instead... *have I unwittingly hurt him so much that I've lost him?*

The car is parked outside the lobby and we get in. We all seem to be feeling tired. Elias takes the front seat, clearly trying to get away from us, and not because he wants to be a good tour guide. He barely speaks to us at all. I lean into

Gino's shoulder, and even Helio puts his arm around me until we think better of showing even more affection and restrain ourselves, not wanting to rub salt in the wound.

This is going to be a long day.

20
ELIAS

I can't stop thinking about what I saw last night. It hurt – catching them all together like that – and all the pain is twisted up with fear and sadness that I can't quite explain.

I don't even want to look at the others on the car journey. I don't want to be here at all.

It's not just that I'm feeling left out, jealous and betrayed all at the same time; there's something else, something more complex.

I want Mira. That's front and center in my mind as usual, but now I also have these other feelings that I wasn't quite expecting… feelings for Gino that I wasn't aware of before.

Sure, I knew there was something between us, but as the car winds through the familiar streets of Athens and then out into the country side, I'm bombarded by more emotions that I can't describe or explain or express. I've lost my ability to think clearly, or to speak. That's when it hits me: this is shame.

I grew up with a lot of homophobia around… and even though I don't care if other people are gay, I seem to have internalized it into myself somehow… and I don't know how to deal with it.

I want Mira all to myself, right now… regardless of how strong I thought I was in the past, regardless of how much I insisted that was the way it was meant to be – that we were all meant to be with Mira… Right now, all I want is for it to just be her and me, living in a cottage somewhere, growing our own vegetables and making our own cheese and cooking… That kind of life is her dream too, I know. She told me once.

Despite how good that fantasy sounds, I know I'm hiding from the truth – Mira really does need to be with all of us, and we need that too… and I know I'm also hiding from my feelings for Gino. My desire for him is dark and strong and insatiable. It scares me. I could get swept up in him, get lost, lose my self… it would change me irrevocably, yes. And that's always scared me, but what scares me more is that I think I'd like it.

I'm not ready to deal with my feelings for Gino. I wish I'd sat into the back seat now, so I could hold tight to Mira in the car, gently pulling her into me, and away from Helio… Helio, who still probably smells like her since I doubt the filthy bastard bothered to shower this morning.

After about half an hour, Helio says he needs to take a piss. The driver pulls into a service station and Mira excuses herself too. I get out of the car, not wanting to be in there with Gino, but he gets out too and steps towards me. I've never wanted to simultaneously hit and kiss anyone as much as I do right now. It makes my blood boil that I can't do either.

There's a look in Gino's eyes. He reaches out towards me, but I turn away, and Gino, who is always so cool and collected, deflates in a way I've only seen once before – the night I rejected him and gave his ring back, all those years ago.

He is crushed, and it crushes me to be the one doing this, especially since there's so much that has shifted between us recently.

Why wasn't I invited...?

That's when I realize it's more complicated than I thought. I'm not just jealous of both guys being with Mira, I'm jealous that Helio was there with Gino as well.

"I'm sorry," Gino says. "... for what you saw last night. It just kind of happened."

The complex emotions rise up like bile inside me. I don't want to see Gino or look at him or any of them, not even Mira, not now... it hurts too much. I want to be alone, back in my garden in El Cielo, but I'm stuck here on this trip in my own home country, and they need me to be their guide.

"Don't..." I say, turning away from Gino.

"Wait," Gino says. "There's something else I have to tell you, and it's not about us. Mira is at risk."

I turn back towards Gino. "What is it?"

"Her ex is after her again. He knows about this trip somehow despite all my precautions, and he's followed us to Greece. The security detail caught sight of him near where we had dinner."

"Shit," I say, panic coursing through my chest. "Are you sure, man?"

Gino looks me in the eye. "I don't want to alarm Mira, but I had to tell her… last night. I don't want to keep secrets from her. It's not worth the risk… I was trying to distract her, to comfort her… but then Helio heard us and…"

I nodded. It makes more sense now. Gino was trying to help Mira feel better after hearing the news and then, as Gino said, it 'just kind of happened'… If I was the one who heard, then it might have been Gino and I and Mira… and Helio as well. Watching Helio jog back to the car, it strikes me that I'm probably not ready for that… not yet.

"Mira doesn't realize how serious it is," Gino says. "But the security guys are worried, and that's bad."

I nod again. "Just let me know if there's anything I can do," I say, because protecting Mira is more important than any jealousy or rage or pain or shame or confusion I might be feeling.

Gino smiles at me, and I feel a surprising warmth spreading through my body followed by a tingling sensation. It's a bit like infatuation, but sweeter, deeper. I take a deep breath, but I don't push it away this time. I let it linger, like the taste of honey, as we get back into the car.

Helio takes the front seat this time, and I get in next to Mira with Gino on the other side. Mira smiles at me hopefully, and I pull her towards me, so that her head rests on my shoulder. My arm wraps around her, coming to rest on her hip, just inches away from Gino. I can practically feel the tension in the electrons in the air between us.

21
MIRA

"Here we are," Gino says.

I look out the window, but all I can see is buildings. We are in a kind of cul-de-sac. It looks like an industrial area.

The car pulls over and we all get out. Gino passes me my backpack, and I take it even though the location doesn't look promising. I doubt this will be a long visit.

Gino stares straight ahead to what looks like a mid-century factory.

"It's… it's all gone," I say, not able to hide my disappointment. I had expected that things would have changed in a couple thousand years, sure, but I hadn't expected this.

Elias wraps his arms around me, comforting me as Gino and Helio take off in different directions, scouting the area.

"Not what you expected?" Elias asks.

"No… I… I mean… what did you think would be here?"

Elias shrugs. "Greece has changed a lot, even just in my lifetime. There used to be more countryside, and now there are buildings everywhere… so many buildings. This land is old – civilization here goes back millennia, but the history gets covered-over with progress, again and again."

"Where did you grow up? I ask. Elias must have told me before, but I can't remember what he said. "Not Athens?"

"No!" Elias laughs, "Nowhere near Athens. We would just sometimes visit on holidays – no. I grew up on an island… actually it's not too far from here."

"What island?" I ask.

"It's called Hydra," Elias says.

"What's it like?"

"It's beautiful," Elias says. "I'd like to take you there sometime if we ever get the chance."

"I'd like that," I say, leaning into him. It's so good to have Elias back in a good mood. The light has returned to his eyes when he looks at me. I don't know what Gino said to him, but it certainly snapped him out of his funk. There's something else in his expression though, something serious… *concern*.

"Over here!" I hear Gino calling.

Elias and I run towards the sound of Gino's voice.

"What?" I ask, catching sight of Gino, around the back of the factory building in a clear grassy space beyond the paved area. I can see some trees spreading out to one side, and there's something about the lay of the land... definitely something familiar about this place, although it's not the forests of my dreams.

I feel a kind of déjà vu.

"There!" Gino says, pointing towards the trees.

I feel their presence before I see them... The sight of the white marble pillars through the scraggly trees sends tingles down my spine.

"The ruins of the temple," Elias says.

Gino nods. Helio runs over, his long black hair streaming out behind him. I can tell he's much happier here despite the industrial wasteland surrounding us. He's more himself than he was in Athens... He seemed so grumpy and listless there, except for that wild time we shared with Gino on the balcony. I'm so pleased that we are all on the same page again, all ourselves, and happy... or at least, happy enough... even though Theo is miles away.

Helio catches up to us and we make our way over towards the ruins together as one group. There is something palpable between us, as if an invisible rope is holding us together, connecting us.

We make our way in formation, like a flock of wild birds, towards the site where we once knew each other before, many years ago. It's such a strange sensation. There are only a few columns remaining of the old temple and some of them are broken. Most of the stone platform below is still visible too, though, even from a distance I can tell it's cracked and worn away by the centuries. There are weeds and little trees trying to burrow their way through the stone, gradually returning everything back to dust, to earth, to the nature that it all came from to begin with.

It's not the nature that bothers me; it's all the newer human-made monstrosities that surround it.

"I can't believe they let people build factories all around here," I say. "Shouldn't it be protected?" I feel angry all of a sudden.

"Eh," Elias shrugs. "It's like I said. This whole country is a historic site. If all the places like this were protected there would be nowhere left for people to live or work. It would just be a big dead museum."

I can kind of see his point, but this place in particular still feels so significant to me. As I near the pillars, my whole body feels suddenly tired and heavy.

"Are you okay, Mira?" Gino asks.

"I'm fine," I say. "I just need a bit of quiet time. I want to sit down under a tree or something. You guys, go, explore."

"Are you sure?" Elias asks.

"Yeah, just promise to tell me what you find."

I walk towards the largest remaining stand of trees. Though I'm sure they're not the exact same trees from our past life here, there's something comforting and familiar about them. I even spot a small stream that must have once been the river… our river. I find a nice big olive tree and sit down underneath it. I watch as the guys excitedly scamper about the ruins, calling out to each other. My eyelids are feeling heavy. My whole body is heavy. I lie back against the tree and let my eyes close for a moment, but then the exhaustion takes me, carrying me away, gently at first, and then swiftly, like a strong current, into a different state of consciousness.

22
MIRA

It looks like... stars... all around me, glimmering, glorious... but I have a feeling they are not stars at all. I don't know where I am now, but it's different, lighter... I feel so... connected... I'm with my others; they are glowing and beautiful, and when I look at them, I realize they are my guys – Theo and Gino and Elias and Helio... just in a different form... our true form?

We are moving, floating towards a large crystalline structure.

A glowing being comes towards us... I can tell it's Micah... beautiful Micah... my guide... A tingle of arousal courses through me, but then I see he's accompanied by another being... I can tell she's an elder soul from her energy. She's so wise. The light shining out from her is deep blue, tinged with purple.

"This is Eliora," Micah says. "She specializes in helping with the life selection process."

She leads us inside. It looks like a small amphitheater, but floating in space with large translucent screens all around. We are here to choose our life... only, it's not this life in modern times. She shows us options, in Ancient Rome, and China, and Egypt, but we choose Greece. It's the one that feels right this time... that will give us the most opportunity to be together in the physical form.

Eliora adjusts the settings to focus on that life. This is her specialization... she helps people to choose their next lives and gives them clues to look out for.

I see myself as Mya, young and innocent, and transfixed by the temple. That is the first sign I must look out for. The temple will stand out for me in this lifetime, and I have to follow my gut. Each of the guys will stand out for me, too. I catch a glimpse of how I first see them. Helio as Teris the blacksmith at his forge, looking hot. Amedes, who is now Theo, outside the temple... my priest. Alfio, Gino, near the herb garden. Lasonas, my Elias, when I've hurt my hand and Alfio takes me to see the doctor. I see flashes of all these things.

"They are special moments," Eliora tells us, showing us each different key points in our lives from our own perspective.

"You want to be together, physically in this life... all of you," she says, and there is no judgement there at all.

Perhaps souls do not judge.

"This is your opportunity for advancement." She shows us another familiar scene: the night of the Mysteries... where we drink the special potion that is said to bring about visions. We are all there, together, at the temple, and the night is free and wild... anything could happen...

"Mira?"

Someone is calling me away from the soft, lightness of this place...

It feels like I'm falling, contracting into the tightness of physical form... disconnecting from all this wonder...

"Mira, are you okay?"

It's Elias' voice. I open my eyes to find myself under the tree near the temple ruins.

"I think I know where we went wrong," I say the guys as they gather around me.

* * *

"What the hell are you talking about?" Helio asks. Subtlety has never been his strong point.

"I'm talking about us," I say. "In the Ancient Greek life – I saw us."

"We've all had the dreams, Mira," Gino says, his perfect brow furrowing in confusion.

"No... this was different," I say, getting up and brushing the dust and leaves off my jeans.

"What do you mean?" Elias asks, reaching out for me. I let him take my hand, but I don't feel all that cuddly. I've just seen something special... magical... other-worldly.

"I think I was in the spirit world," I say.

"What?" all three of the guys ask at once.

I nod. "Yes... or at least, I was in a memory of it, but it was more than just a memory because it was like I was myself here, but looking back on us all choosing a life, thousands of years ago... How can that be possible?"

Gino's eyes light up with something like awareness. "That

makes sense," he says. "Time doesn't exist there… not in the same way that it does here… so, if you have a memory or an experience in the spirit world, it's like you are in all places at once, though your perspective is concentrated on one point more than others…"

"That's exactly what it was like," I say, surprised that Gino was able to capture my experience so well with his words.

"Mira," Elias says, interlocking my fingers between his. "You just said you found out what went wrong with us in that lifetime. What was it? What did you see?"

"You were right," I say to the guys. "You were all right; we are meant to be together – intimately…"

"Like a big orgy?" Helio asks.

I laugh. "Kind of… yeah. It sounds weird, but I think the sex is part of our purpose here."

"That sounds… convenient," Helio says and laughs.

"I get the feeling that sex is something that requires the physical world to experience it properly… just like food." I say.

Gino nods, "Yes, as I understand it, Mira is right. These are some of the pinnacles of experience of physical life."

"You're saying we came to Earth to fuck?" Helio says, clearly finding this amusing.

"No, but I do think that being together physically is part of what *we* need to do…"

It sounds ridiculous when I put it like that, and for a moment, I wonder if I've got this all wrong.

"I've had similar realizations, Mira," Gino says, reassuring me. "It seems like it's part of our advancement as souls… with overcoming our egos… It's part of what we are meant to be doing here.

"Exactly," I say, "And that's what I saw in my vision, or whatever that was. There was one night in particular when we all could have been together…"

"The Mysteries," says Elias.

I nod.

"You're right," Gino says. "We were free… we could have done anything we wanted under the spell of the gods… but we messed it up because of our own fears and failings…"

"We lost our chance…" Elias says, sadly.

"What are you trying to tell us, Mira?" Helio asks, impatiently. "What do you want?"

"I want to try it again," I say. "But I want to do it right this time. I want a banquet like the Mysteries… With all of us, and Theo as well. I want to reconstruct it somehow… figure out what was in that potion."

I want all of them.

The guys around me look baffled and intrigued, and more than a little bit interested.

Elias scratches his head, deep in thought. "It's like you're psychic or something."

"What do you mean?"

"You could see the ghost when none of us could, you could talk to her in your dreams, and now you can just pop into the spirit world for a quick visit…"

He's looking at me in awe. I smile, feeling a bit stunned by the suggestion.

"There is something special about you, Mira," Gino says.

Just then, a gust of wind blows through the trees surrounding us and another sound emerges. It's Gino's phone ringing. He answers it. His posture changes, becomes rigid. Something is wrong. He speaks in very fast Italian and then hangs us.

"We've got to get out of here," Gino says, looking at me.

"Cliff?"

He nods.

I shudder.

"I don't know how, but he's followed us this far."

"I bet it was Inara," I say. *I knew I didn't like that woman, right from the start...*

"Why are you so suspicious of Inara?" Gino asks, raising an eyebrow. "I told you, she's a trusted employee."

"Is it possible, though?" I ask. "She may have been in a position to ask the driver… to make inquiries before we left about our itinerary."

"I guess it's possible," Gino admits.

"Well, whoever it is feeding information to Cliff, it's not good news. What are we going to do?" I ask.

"I could just kick his ass for you, Mira," Helio says. "Please let me punch him. It would be so satisfying…"

"It's too much of a risk," I say. "He's unpredictable and dangerous… especially when he gets fixated on something."

"I'm sure the three of us could take him," Helio scoffs.

I look from him to the other guys, and I don't doubt that

they're strong and absolutely dedicated to protecting me, but it's not worth the risk.

I shake my head. "I'm not willing to take the risk…"

"Remember how much he's hurt Mira in the past," Elias says. "She doesn't want to see him – to relive the trauma."

"Then let's get the fuck out of here," Helio says.

"How?" I ask. "The driver might be in-league with Cliff, for all we know."

Gino looks stumped. It's rare for him to be the silent one, but the mystery of how Cliff is following us is obviously bothering him. He paces back and forth, as if processing all the possibilities.

"There's a port," Elias suggests. "I saw it from down at the edge of the river. It's probably five minutes away."

"You want us to leave the car, and all our things?" Gino asks.

"It's the best bet," Helio says. "You can't guarantee you can trust the driver."

"And then what?" I ask.

"We lie low for a few days," Helio says. "Elias will tell us where to go."

"I know just the place," Elias says.

23
MIRA

Gino calls the driver and tells him to drive back to Athens without us, and then he turns to look at us. "Alright. Let's go."

We take off, running down through the ruins of the temple to the end of the river, and towards the port in the distance. It takes longer than five minutes, but I'm not complaining. It feels good that the guys are all on my side, protecting me from Cliff. There's a port filled with boats, but no obvious boat hire places. The guys don't seem concerned. Gino and Elias walk up to a couple of old men on the jetty and talk to them in Greek. I didn't even know Gino could speak Greek, but he sounds fluent.

"What's going on?" I ask Helio.

"They're figuring it out," he replies.

"What do you mean?"

"If you want to know anything about a place, all you have to do is ask old people. They know it all."

The next thing I know, Gino is on the phone, apparently sorting out details to hire the fastest boat in the port. Less than ten minutes later, a middle-aged man wearing a half open silk shirt is leading us down to a big, expensive looking boat.

He shows us around on-board, there are several bedrooms down below that look just like hotel suites, and a big lounge, surrounded by dark mahogany paneling and carpeted in royal blue shag so thick that my feet sink right into it. I could get used to this. There's even a big kitchen, and a bar, presumably set up for catering functions.

I have no idea how much it's costing us to hire this floating mansion at short notice but Gino gives silk-shirt guy a big wad of cash before he leaves. He smiles and winks at us.

Can he can tell we're into group sex... or is that just my imagination?

Once the boat guy leaves, Helio takes charge of the ship, taking a seat behind the wheel and examining the complicated-looking dials and screens in front of him. He looks as if he's totally at home in the cockpit, and it takes a lot of self-control for me not to make a stupid joke about that.

"I know Helio's an engineer," I say to Gino, "but does he know what he's doing?"

Gino smiles. "Helio's very experienced, he even has a captain's license."

These guys are always so full of surprises... of course one of them has a captain's license... as if that's quite a normal thing to have.

Elias helps Helio navigate towards wherever it is he says is the perfect place for us to go. I'm aware that there are a lot of Greek islands, but I've never been to any of them before.

As the boat pulls away from the port and speeds off towards the horizon, I feel a thrill of excitement – it's the feeling of taking flight on a new adventure… but at the same time, there's a sadness growing inside me that I wish I could leave behind, and it has everything to do with Theo not being here with us.

"You look like you could do with a drink," Gino says and heads towards the bar.

I walk out onto the deck and survey the horizon. It's so stunningly blue – the sea fading into the perfectly clear sky. I get lost in it for a moment, then Gino appears at my side again, holding a drink in a martini glass. I give him a suspicious look, remembering how we first met. He knows damn well I can't stand martinis. He breaks into a big grin. "Relax, it's Ouzo and lemon."

I want to give him a playful shove for teasing me like this, but I don't want to spill the drink. I just glare at him instead, prompting him to chuckle.

I take a sip of the tart, spicy drink. Ouzo is definitely growing on me. "I could get used to this," I say, staring out to the horizon again.

"It's beautiful, no?" Gino says, wrapping his arm around me. I lean into him, inhaling the scent of his expensive cologne. I thought I'd sworn off wealthy men after Cliff, but meeting Gino changed all that for me. He and Theo both prefer the more refined things in life, although they are both quite different in their tastes, while my other guys, Elias and Helio, like to keep things simple... also in very different ways.

Remembering Theo's absence brings another pang of sadness.

"You are missing him, aren't you," Gino says. His mind-reading habit is getting out of control.

"Yeah," I sigh. "Do you?"

"In a manner of speaking. We all have a strong bond – the four of us."

"But you and Elias..." We've never properly talked about the intimacy between these two, but I can tell it's there, even if I've seen them both deny it at times and turn away from each other.

"It's different between us," Gino says. "You can tell, can't you?"

I nod. "Something seems to be changing... recently."

Gino has a tight-lipped smile, and I can tell what he's thinking this time: *I hope so... it's too early to tell.*

"Is that okay with you?" he asks. "Elias and I..."

"Of course it is," I say. "It's actually kind of hot."

Gino laughs, "I'm glad you think so. Your wellbeing is so important to both of us."

Gino's voice is edged with concern.

"Do you think Cliff will try to follow us?" I ask.

Gino shrugs, "It would be difficult for him to chase us out to sea," he says. "And he doesn't know where we're going."

"We can't keep running forever," I say. "Lana is always accusing me of running away. She thinks I should face him."

"And what do you think?"

"Maybe she's right. I mean, if he's following us now, and he clearly knows about El Cielo since he's been sending all those creepy packages, what's to stop him from showing up there at any time?"

"We have security protecting the retreat," Gino says. "I expect Cliff will get worse for a while, and then he'll give up."

"What makes you say that?" I ask. *What does Gino know that he's not telling me?*

"Just a suspicion," Gino says. "I've got some plans underway. It's to do with getting Cliff out of the company, but don't worry about the details for now. I'll tell you everything in due course, but you can relax, Mira. We're here for you. We'll protect you."

The rest of the voyage goes smoothly. I wouldn't mind staying on the boat all night, but Elias has other plans, and anyway, while the bar is well stocked, there's no food in the kitchen. We pull into the port of a small island.

"Where are we?" I ask Elias.

"This is the place we call Alos," he replies. "It's where my grandmother grew up."

"I thought we were going to Hydra," I say. "Isn't that where you said you're from?"

"I thought that might be too obvious," Elias says. "Clifford Maxwell won't trace us here. He might seek us out on Hydra because as you say, it's where I grew up… but this connection is untraceable."

I still feel uneasy. I know better than to underestimate Cliff. When we were together, I saw the ruthless way he treated his enemies.

"Can't we just pick up some supplies and stay on the boat?" I ask him.

"The weather report is predicting a storm later," Gino says. "I'd prefer to sleep on land."

"Where will we stay?" I ask, imagining Gino has another hotel in mind, but from the looks of the simple fishing village, there aren't many fancy accommodations on the island.

"I've just hired us a small house for the night," Gino says, holding up his phone.

I shrug, still feeling uneasy, but not wanting to argue with the guys after they've gone to all this trouble. I begin to relax more as we leave the boat and walk along the jetty towards the picturesque town.

Alos is beautiful. The rounded white-washed houses with their cobalt blue doors and window trim against the perfect cloudless sky, and the ombre shading of the azure ocean, fading from turquoise to deep navy.

I sigh at the beauty of it all.

"So much blue," I say, to Elias.

"They say you don't understand the color blue until you visit Greece." He grins at me.

"Maybe they're right."

Elias leads us to the market where he buys fresh fish and

bread and vegetables. Gino buys wine from a local merchant, then we follow him up a steep track as we navigate towards the house he booked, walking along the gorgeous cobbled lanes between the whitewashed houses with their blue trim. Purple bougainvillea hangs in thick boughs over trellises, the only thing in sight that breaks away from the white and blue color scheme of the island, as if it doesn't give a damn.

We only have a couple of backpacks and satchels between us, as the rest of our luggage is back at the hotel. I'm glad I threw a change of clothes into mine this morning, wondering if I'd need to wear something fancier later in the day. It's a burgundy silk dress with thin shoulder straps, and an open back. I don't think we are going to be doing any fine dining on this small island that is magically remote enough to avoid the tourist routes that have ruined many other Greek islands. Still, I expect that Gino would have hired the fanciest, most modern holiday home on the island. I'm pleasantly surprised to find it's just as quaint and rustic as everything else here.

As soon as we arrive, I know it's perfect. There's no way in hell Cliff could find us here. Not only is this island blissfully isolated, this house is totally indistinguishable from any other house here with its whitewashed exterior and cobalt blue shutters.

As Gino finds the hidden key and lets us in, a cold breeze breaks through and I look up to see storm clouds rolling in overhead. I'm grateful that we didn't stay on the boat tonight. It looks like quite a storm brewing despite the perfectly clear day we had.

The room has plain stone floors, with soft rugs, and a fire place, which seems like it might come in handy with the sudden drop in temperature from the weather changing.

Elias heads straight for the simple kitchen in the corner of the large open plan living area. He immediately begins slicing up tomatoes and bread from the market, and I suddenly realize how famished I am. I steal a crust of bread and drizzle some olive oil over it because I can't wait to eat. I devour the delicious rustic sourdough and reach for more.

Meanwhile, Gino has found the record player in the corner on the room and put on some gentle Greek acoustic guitar music.

My eyes pan the room, seeking out Helio. I notice he's opened the doors out to the balcony, and despite the brewing storm, he's out there, looking at the beginnings of what promises to be a spectacular sunset if the clouds don't close in too fast.

I follow Helio outside, still scoffing my bread. He looks so gorgeous, standing there that I can't help but wrap my arm around him.

"Food?" Helio asks.

"Yes – food!" I turn to see Elias is already carrying out a large platter of bread, sliced tomatoes, basil, olives, feta cheese and salami. It's a quick and easy antipasto, and it's exactly what we all need right now. Gino opens a bottle of wine, and we all dig in. Despite the chill in the air and the promise of rain, there's something thick and delicious about the atmosphere here, tonight, something electric that sends a shiver down my spine, and I think about all the delicious things I could do with my guys. I'm enjoying everything about this until Helio brings up Cliff again.

"I don't get it," Helio says. "Clifford Maxwell obviously knows El Cielo. He keeps sending you creepy mail. If he knows where we live, why the hell is he chasing us now?"

"I was wondering that, myself," I reply.

"It's a power game and we won't let him win," Gino says.

"But isn't he winning if we're running from him?" Helio asks. "Why won't you let us kick his ass, Mira?"

"It's too dangerous," I say, shivering, only partly due to the cold breeze. Elias takes his jacket off and wraps it around my shoulders.

"He doesn't know we're running from him," Gino says. "He thinks he has outsmarted us – following us without us knowing about him. Our security detail is hard to detect."

"But Inara…" I start to say.

"We're not sure it was her, Mira," Gino interrupts. "But there is clearly some weakness that I hadn't counted on. If Clifford Maxwell is going to play it like this, then perhaps I have no choice."

"What do you mean?" I ask.

"I've had Cliff investigated. As you know, trying to get him out of the company," Gino says. "They've dug up some dirt on him. It's a sex scandal with an underaged girl in Amsterdam from ten years ago. It's enough to land him in jail and ruin his businesses."

My stomach churns. "Isn't that something he should be

charged for anyway?" I ask. "I mean... I can see how it's useful to us to kind of... blackmail him, but..."

"You're right, Mira," Gino says. "The only problem is that it will probably be hard for the police to pin it on him after so much time has elapsed. It might provide enough leverage though, to get him out of El Cielo and the company as a shareholder first, and then we can hand the information over to the Dutch police and see if anything comes of it."

"How the hell did Mira's ex get involved in your company and invest in El Cielo, anyway?" Helio asks. "That's some fucking coincidence."

"I don't believe it is," Gino says.

"I've been wondering about that," I add. "I get that we are repeating lives together, but Victor didn't know about his past life connection. I've been wondering if maybe Cliff does..."

"You mean, it was deliberate?" Elias asks.

"Isn't is too much of a coincidence?" I reply. "I think he must have somehow tracked you guys down before he met me."

"So, getting in on the business was his way of staying in the know about what's going on... kind of monitoring the place?" Helio asks.

I nod, shivering with the implications of all this. "It's like he did everything he could to keep me locked away, and after I left, maybe he was still watching me, waiting for me to fail and come back to him, but it was only after I met Gino and came to El Cielo that Cliff started obviously stalking me..."

"Get that creep out of your mind, Mira," Elias says, refilling my wine glass. "You're here with us and it's a beautiful night. Let's celebrate."

Just then, Gino's phone rings. He stands up and walks away to answer it and when he comes back, he has a strange expression on his face.

"What is it?" I ask.

"Update from my security guys," Gino says. "Apparently, Clifford Maxwell got to the temple site a few hours after us."

"What happened?" Helio asks. I can tell from his tone that he's disappointed he wasn't there to confront Cliff.

"The security guys say he walked out there, and straight away, he crumpled down to his knees and started crying."

"What?" I say. "I've never seen him cry before." Even the thought of it is unnerving. "Maybe it was the site of the temple… maybe it affected him somehow."

"Where has he gone now?" Helio asks.

"They think he's heading back to Athens," Gino says.

"That's a shame," Helio says. "I was really hoping to have a chance to punch him in the face."

As reassuring as it is to have Helio wanting to stand up for me, I still don't want us confronting Cliff. He's too dangerous, even with four against one. It's not Cliff's size or his strength that frightens me. It's his absolute determination, his callousness, his lack of regard for anything other than getting what he wants. I also know that he always finds a way to carry a gun, and the last thing I need is any of my guys dying… again. *We've got to get it right this lifetime.*

I push my fears about my stalkerish creep of an ex out of

THE SIGHT OF SEA AND SPIRIT

my mind. It feels like I've been whisked away, from one paradise at El Cielo to another on Alos, watching the gorgeous tangerine sky as the sun sets over the ocean. I could live here. It's perfect... but of course, I'd need all the guys with me and we wouldn't all fit in this little cottage, at least not for long, and then there's Theo to consider. Thinking of him makes me feel sad... and also aroused... especially after our last encounter.

We enjoy our time out on the balcony with wine and snacks, but it's not long before the rain closes in on us. We each grab plates and glasses and quickly dash away from the big raindrops splashing all around. Lightning strikes, and a few moments later, the thunder sounds as the storm rolls in. I look out towards the darkening sky and sea as Elias busies himself in the kitchen again.

"I need a shower," Helio says, giving me a look that tempts me to join him. I decide not to rock the boat and risk upsetting Elias again, but I do feel grubby, so I take a quick shower after Helio, and throw on the silk dress from my backpack. It's somehow only slightly creased. I don't even bother with a bra since we're clearly not going anywhere tonight.

By the time I'm out, dinner is ready, and Helio is lighting the fire. Elias has made fresh fish, pan-seared with capers and lemon, with grilled eggplants, peppers and tomatoes. It's a perfect and delicious meal: simple, fresh, and tasty.

Gino puts on gentler guitar music, and Helio sighs dramatically. "Can't you find something with a little more energy?"

"I don't know Greek music," Gino shrugs.

"Then let the Greek guy choose," Helio says, showing Elias in the direction of the record player, who chuckles and then selects a different record. It's more intense and passionate and reminds me a bit of the man playing music in the Greek restaurant.

"That's better," Helio says.

I've had a couple of glasses of wine by now and find myself swaying with the music. Helio pulls me up to stand beside him.

"Oh, no," I say. "I can't really dance."

"You can," Gino argues. "We danced in the rain, remember?"

"That was different," I say. "That wasn't really dancing. When I actually try to dance, I have two left feet, and I just kind of stumble over myself."

"Rubbish," Helio says, taking my hand and twirling me around. "Everyone can dance."

"That might be so," I say. "But I'm not sure everyone should… I mean, it's not really my thing…"

But despite my protestations, it seems I am dancing already, and Helio's broad smile is infectious. Helio spins me again, right into Gino, who holds me close and slow as we sway together. It's so sexy I practically swoon into his arms, and then something catches his eye. Elias is standing a few feet away, watching us. Gino takes my hand and leads me towards him. Elias actually knows how to dance to this music, and he takes the lead, guiding me around the room. I barely have to think, I just let go and follow his steps.

"See," Helio says, triumphantly. "You *can* dance."

I laugh, not expecting to agree with him on this, and still not a hundred percent convinced that what I'm doing is dancing, until I catch sight of us in the mirror on the far wall. Elias twirls me, elegantly, and then draws me close.

"Maybe I just needed the right dance partners." I say.

Elias leads me to Gino, who gracefully dances me around the room and then back to Helio, and we start the cycle again. It's fun, and flirtatious, and very, very sexy. I find myself all worked up, with dampness building between my thighs.

I watch Elias' face as we dance to make sure he's okay, and thankfully, he's totally into it, especially with all the attention I'm giving him... *maybe this dancing is going to get me exactly where I want to be right now.*

I give Elias what I hope is a seductive look as I dance with Helio, then gently push Helio away, in a flirtatious way and strut towards Elias letting my hips swing in time to the music. I pull him towards me, my breasts brush against his chest. It feels so good – my nipples rubbing against the silk fabric, leaning into Elias and inhaling his perpetually herby, musky scent.

His hands are all over me, stroking down my back and over my ass, lifting the hem of my dress and caressing my thighs, and then stroking my nipples through the thin silky fabric. *Mmmmm...*

For a moment I forget where I am, and then I glance around at the others. Both Gino and Helio are only a few feet away, staring at me as if I'm something to eat, and that's exactly what I intend to be.

I give them an inviting look, and then turn back to Elias. He grasps the hair at be base of my neck, firmly but smoothly, and then pulls me into a kiss. I'm hoping that Helio and Gino will take my cue and join in, and my hopes are realized when I feel two more pairs of satisfying hands begin to stroke my back, my arms, my thighs... *this is really happening... I'm in heaven, kissing Elias while Helio and Gino caress me.*

A moment later, Elias pulls away, then he grasps my waist firmly and begins kissing me right down my neck and then down my chest. I can feel everything through the thin fabric of my dress. He looks up at me, seeking my consent. I smile at him and put my hands on his shoulders... *yes... please.*

Elias lifts my dress and rolls my panties down to the floor, allowing me to step out of them... then he dives into me, eating my pussy as if it's a delectable three course meal. I groan in pleasure and immediately feel the other guy's hands tighten against me. Clearly, I'm turning them both on, and I want this to go on and on and on...

Elias sucks on my clit, groaning into me, sending vibrations through me. I can barely stand up through the waves of pleasure, I lean back against Gino and feel his hard cock press between my butt cheeks. I've never been interested in anal before this moment. But right now, I want it all.

I push my butt back, nudging Gino's cock further. *Mmm...*

I cup the back of Gino's head with my hand and whisper, "it feels so good," sliding back even further into him as he rubs some of my juices up, moistening places where no one else has touched.

THE SIGHT OF SEA AND SPIRIT

Helio leans in, his scent is intoxicating, wild woodsmoke. He slips the thin straps from my shoulders, freeing my breasts. He rolls the palms of his hands around them, giving them a squeeze just as Elias slips one finger inside my pussy, and then another.

I moan again, with a growing longing to be filled completely. I reach for Helio, pulling him into a deep, intense kiss while my other hand wanders down towards his pants, to the hard cock standing at attention, just waiting for me to stroke it...

As Elias flicks his fingers inside me, against my g-spot, my legs buckle. The pleasure is too intense. I step back from Elias and kick the large ottoman over towards the sofa, then I pull Elias up to standing and gently push him back against the soft furnishings... *yes... this will do nicely.*

I may have spent a little while researching group sex positions on google in my spare time...

I pounce on Elias and his eyes light up. Then I unbuckle his belt and slide his pants off. I have him exactly where I want him. I unbutton his linen shirt and then take off my dress completely. We are both stark naked while the others are fully clothed... but not for long. I beckon them both over, pulling them both in close. "I want you to take off your clothes," I say, "and stay close." Then, as Helio scrambles to get his pants off, I whisper to Gino, telling him exactly what I want him to do to me.

Gino disappears, returning moments later with a bottle of olive oil. In the meantime, I turn my attention back to Elias, running my hands over his chest. As I'm lying on top of him, I can feel his shaft sliding between the lips of my pussy. I grind into it, making him groan in pleasure. Then, I lift myself up, position him below my entrance, and lower myself onto his cock. He feels so fucking good that I get lost in the sensation – his cock sliding inside me, his hands reaching up to stroke my breasts.

It's almost as if I cease to exist amid all this sensation… there is only pleasure… only bliss.

Then I feel Gino behind me, fulfilling my wicked plan. I hear the bottle being opened and then the cold sensation as the oil slides between my butt cheeks. The rush of anticipation through me, prompts me to reach for Helio's enormous cock, stroking it with my hands, up and down the shaft, as I continue to ride Elias, rhythmically. Meanwhile behind me, Gino begins to smear the olive oil, mingling with my own juices, that have been practically dripping down my thighs, around my other opening. I feel his finger nudge into me, gently, probing me, and the need to be filled even more overtakes me.

I take Helio into my mouth, as Gino adds another finger. I'm insatiable. Everything must be filled.

Gino gently pushes me forwards and I drag Helio with me, jostling him over towards the side of the sofa. Gino positions himself behind me, his knee on the ottoman, as my whole body loosens for him. It's such an intense, unusual underwater feeling. Bubbles of pleasure explode though me as Gino's cock slides slowly into my ass, rubbing up against the pressure building from Elias, from the other side.

Oh... my... gods...

It's almost too much. The intensity is overwhelming for a moment. I'm pushing up against my own wall of resistance, my fear, my trauma, but instead of running, instead of breaking away from it and abandoning the guys in full swing, I take a deep breath, focusing only on the physical sensations of my body: pleasure, pain, arousal, delight, and longing... and then I lean into the fear and find an even deeper pleasure.

My whole body feels like it's vibrating, humming in delicious desire and ecstasy. We are all moaning, panting, groaning, together as one, like a multi-headed beast. The momentum builds, just as the pressure does, from all angles. The orgasm hits me so hard it seems to transmute reality.

It's like magic. A sudden change comes over us, as if we are transported into sacred space, as if we are out of time. I can still see the room around us, but it looks like it's hazy, as If I'm looking through a mist, as if I can see the atoms in the air, as if we're floating high above in the atmosphere... as if the only thing that exists are these beautiful godly male beings around me. They seem to glow, as if they're etheric... supernatural.

Elias groans beneath me, arching up, thrusting deeper onto me, grounding me back into the physical with the sensation of pleasurable pain. It's building... expanding inside of me, through me, a wave so intense it threatens to swallow us all whole. I reach for Helio's balls, holding them and finding that pressure point behind them that I know he loves. The wave rocks through him… through all of us. Gino and Elias lock hands, and I can see a circle of light emanating out from their interlaced fingers, forming a circle around me… It's just like a magic spell… or perhaps just an orgasmic hallucination. Gino shudders behind me, collapsing into me. Just as I feel Elias' release inside me, I'm rocketed into another plane of existence, entirely. The stars at the edges of my vision blanket out until all I can see is white…

24
CLIFF

The night is colder than I expected. The water is black like midnight. It's almost beautiful and certainly makes a compelling background view as I contemplate all the things I could do to Mira.

The rain sets in before long, but I don't care.

All the better to hunt you in, my dear.

As the boat pulls into the port, I laugh to myself. *I bet they think they're safe on this piece of shit island that even the tourists can't be bothered with.*

Back on the mainland, I ducked away from those undercover security guards. I pretended I was headed back to Athens, and then took the first speedboat I could find for hire, in the direction of the beacon on my GPS tracker app.

It was too easy to get that woman, Inara, wound around my little finger a few weeks ago. All I had to do was flick some rolls of hundred-dollar bills around and she was practically begging to suck my cock. It was only a slight diversion, fucking her, and too tempting in that tight jumpsuit she likes to wear. I love a challenge and peeling that thing off her and then fucking her senseless was just the thing to take my mind off my little problem.

Mira... when the fuck did you get so feisty?

It was when she met them, of course. They bring it out of her. That was why I had to have them followed. Inara told me when they were on their way to the airport in Barcelona, and she did a good job of planting that tracking chip on Gino too. I bet she gave him a big hug and kiss and wanted more, that little whore. It's a shame I won't have any more use for her now. She was a good lay.

It was a fun game to play while it lasted.... Sending Mira gifts and imagining how messed up she could get over them, but enough! This has got to end, even if I have to take them all down. Every. Last. One.

I follow the beacon up a winding cobbled pathway. It leads to an innocuous looking house – just the same whitewashed peasant dwelling as everywhere else. It's trash, just like Mira is. I hate her for leaving me, even though she barely provided any challenge in all the years I kept her captive. I even started to wonder what all the fuss was about. *Why does it always come back to her?* Then, after she left, I was done with her, at least so I thought. I kept an eye on her whereabouts... my wayward wife, the little slut, but she didn't interest me much. I'd been there, done that. I was sick of her pathetic ways, sick of how much she wanted to be common, of how whenever I asked her what she wanted, she never asked for diamonds or a nice car, it was always chef school. The little tart wanted to cook, and I was almost ready to leave her to her own devices until she met Gino.

Of course, I found out straight away. I have my ways of knowing these things, and I always keep tabs on what's mine. She might be a stupid little slut, but she's still mine. I tried to stop her taking his offer. I sent her a letter to make her think I was involved, expecting it would be enough of a curve ball to get her running in the opposite direction, I hadn't counted on her tardiness; she didn't even check her letters until weeks later. Too many bills she was avoiding, I guess. That's Mira: always running. Always avoiding.

I can't see anything from the street, so I angle my way around the house, climbing a trellis, and balancing on some old rotting planks of wood, until I can clamber up onto the veranda.

You see... Mira? You see what you made me do? I'm out here like a common peasant, like a petty burglar, in the fucking rain... but it will all be worth it just to get my revenge.

I didn't want it to get this far. I sent her my engagement ring, with the big diamonds she never even liked... nothing. Turns out the little bitch didn't even care about her vows. I sent the ring as a reminder of Mira's commitment and as a warning to them all. Stay away. She's mine.

I can barely see through the misted windows. I get closer

and hold my hands up against the glass, not giving a fuck if they see me now. They're the ones who should be worried.

As I look though, it takes me a while to make out the scene in front of me. They're all fucking naked. *That was not what I was expecting... a motherfucking orgy... well, Mira... turns out you're an even bigger slut than I realized...*

She's riding one of the guys while she sucks another guy's cock – the big one, and the other guy, the only one I know in person, Gino, looks like he's fucking her in the asshole. *Fuck. I never even tried that... she's my wife, for fuck's sake. I fucked plenty of whores in the ass... I certainly never expected this from her.*

I'm filled with rage and it makes me so hard I reach for my own cock, stroking in time with their movements, while I imagine killing each and every one of them

Murder is not usually worth the risk, but anything can disappear for a price. I've seen it many times before, and this definitely calls for extreme measures. The thought of all that blood – that's what gets me off every time. It doesn't take long before I come in my hand.

Oh... yes...

It takes a moment before it occurs to me that something's not right. Mira is on the floor, inside. She's collapsed. The guys are all standing around her, looking tense, as if something's wrong. One of them is checking her pulse...

Well this is another unexpected development...

25
GINO

"Mira!" Elias cries and I'm confused by the tone of panic in his voice... that is, until Mira collapses sideways, falling from Elias, tumbling to the floor.

At first, I think it's a mistake – that she somehow lost her balance – but her eyes are closed despite Elias calling her name over and over, despite us all standing over her, gently shaking her, talking to her...

She's non-responsive.

"Is she..." I start to ask, but for once, I'm rendered speechless. I can't bear to articulate my own fearful thoughts. *Is she okay? Is she alive? Is she d...*

I'm not even going to think it.

"What do we do?" Elias asks, turning to me.

"Aren't you a doctor?" Helio asks Elias.

"That was in a past life, remember!" he responds, sounding panicked. "Things have changed since then."

I reach down and press my fingers to into the side of her neck.

"She has a pulse," I say, breathing a sigh of relief. "It's faint... but I think she's alright. At least, she's alive."

"But... what do we do?" Elias asks, looking at me with those beautiful blue eyes full of pain and fear.

"She probably just fainted," Helio says. "She did that before, remember – with the ghost... that séance thing."

"This was different," Elias says. "This time... it was like she was here one minute and then... gone."

"She'll probably come around in a minute," Helio says, although even *he* doesn't sound too sure.

"Elias was the one in front of her, closest to her when it happened, and if he's worried, I believe him," I say.

"Let's at least get some clothes on her," Elias says. "Hopefully she'll come to, and if she doesn't, she'll be more dressed... you know... if we have to take her to a doctor."

"At this time of night?" Helio asks. "During a storm? Are you serious?"

"Helio's right," Elias says. "It will be hard finding a doctor on this island at this time."

"The storm's dying down," I say. "Maybe we can get her back to the mainland. At least that way, there will be a proper hospital."

We manage to find Mira's dress and pull it over her. She doesn't stir at all. It's like Elias said...

It's like she's gone.

My heart is racing in my chest at the thought. The blood flooding through my veins feels cold and metallic, like mercury.

Mira... we need you to survive, okay? We need you here... please stay with us.

Elias gently cleans Mira up with a towel and a damp face cloth from the bathroom, then he rolls her panties back up her legs. At least now, we won't look too suspicious to any medical professionals we manage to find.

I check Mira's pulse again; it's still very faint, but it's still there.

"You're right," Helio says. It's not something I often hear him say. "The storm is dying down. And you're also right, we should get her to a hospital... just in case..."

We wrap her carefully in blankets from the house. Of course, I'm happy to pay for replacements. I hope the owners aren't attached to these particular ones. It's nothing compared to the other worries weighing on my mind right now. I brush aside every thought that isn't to do with keeping Mira alive, and safe, and well. I find an old rain jacket and cover her with it, then I grab Mira's backpack, in case it contains anything she needs. I'm just hoping like hell she'll still be here, and that she's well enough to need things like lipstick or deodorant.

Helio hoists Mira up, carrying her as if she's light at a feather. I knew there was a reason we kept that guy around.

I love Helio like a brother. Sometimes he's a pain in the ass and arrogant as hell, but right now I'm happy he's here more than ever. Not many people are as strong as him.

I'm sure I see movement from the corner of my eye as we leave the house, but I don't have time to turn back and examine what I assume is just a stray dog or cat anyway.

We take off into the empty lane. Lightning strikes and thunder crashes overhead. We race down through the wind and rain towards the port. The boat sits proudly in front of us, the biggest vessel for miles, and strong enough to weather much bigger storms.

Maybe Mira was right... maybe we should have just stayed aboard the boat, that way we wouldn't have wasted precious time in getting her back down here...

It's not long before we're back on board. I turn the lights on, and Elias is quick to start the engine and get the heating going. Helio takes Mira over to the large sofa to the side of the main room, placing her down gently and even humming what sounds like a lullaby to her as he strokes her hair... well, that's sure a side of Helio I've never seen before, but it's not the right time to compliment him on his maternal instincts, or even tease him about them. I grab another pile of blankets to help keep her warm as the boat slowly warms up.

We are so busy rushing around and tending to Mira that none of us realize a fifth person has entered the boat.

"Ready?" Elias calls out as he prepares the boat to take off.

"I'm ready for anything," the unfamiliar voice says.

I look up to see a man in a rain parka, his hood drawn up

tightly around his face, his blonde hair plastered to his forehead.

It's hardly the time to be dealing with a stray drunk, and then it sinks in... the man's voice is not entirely unfamiliar, after all.

He's no stranger.

The man standing in front of us, grinning maniacally is none other than the last person I want to see right now: Clifford Maxwell.

26
MIRA

Everything is expanding... exponentially... all there is, is connectedness, bliss... a moment ago, I was in the midst of an orgasm... except it just keeps coming, keeps going, I'm floating... higher... higher... I'm high above, looking down on everyone... everything is white...

It's like I've left my body entirely.

Where am I?

As I look around, I realize it's not bright white at all... at least, not anymore. I'm looking out over galaxies of stars... only they're not stars... they're something else, something familiar; I know this intuitively even though I have no idea where I am.

As I stare out into the vast expanse, I feel peace, like I'm part of everything... there's a warm feeling, like a water bed, or a bath that's just the right temperature.

Someone is coming towards me. They are glowing. Beautiful... just like I imagine an angel to be. Only, this angel is familiar, too.

It's my guide.... The realization brings me so much joy. My guide is coming towards me... It's just like in the book I read... It's all real... I know him, I recognize him from all the times I've caught glimpses of him in my mind. I used to think he was an imaginary friend, but now I know for sure that he is so much more. He's always with me... protecting me from harm like a guardian angel.

Then I remember what I was just doing and blush...

Micah laughs... or at least, he seems to laugh... it's kind of like vibrations, like music, like the sound of gentle wind chimes.

There's no judgement here, he reminds me.

What am I doing here? I ask. My voice comes out in the form of vibrations too... I'm quickly realizing that I'm in my body... I'm glowing just like Micah, only he's kind of bluey purply colored, surrounded in golden light, whereas it looks like I'm glowing yellow with specks of blue.

I have a message for you... Micah says. *Your real struggle is within... but there are external goals that will help you to achieve the transformation you require.*

What do you mean? I ask. I don't understand completely, but something flashes in my mind; it's a vision of me and the guys, all together and naked!

The way the physical works is? reflective, Micah replies.

I can sense the truth in the meaning Micah is conveying in

his charm-like voice, but I don't quite understand the connection, and then he holds out his arms towards me, unleashing pure golden light. It's delightful as it tickles through me, bringing me to a new level of understanding. *Are you saying what we do with our bodies relates to our soul development... like a mirror?* I ask.

Yes, and also more like a prism... the light of awareness shines through and splits into all the colors of reality. Whatever you are seeing out there in your life is in some way a reflection, a projection of the inner.

Are you saying it's not real? I ask.

Not at all, Micah replies. *It's certainly real. In fact, it feels more real than this place, doesn't it?*

I reflect on this. *It feels... harder, more condensed, more limited, more solid.*

I can tell Micah is agreeing with me, but he also wants to challenge me more. *In the physical form, we see the manifestation to the most extreme of what can be imagined here. It is the hyperreality we've all created, in which to advance consciousness.*

I'm confused. *What... consciousness...? Are you saying life is just a simulation, like a video game? But that means all the terrible things that happen are planned... All the wars and murders and atrocities?*

When you say game, it trivializes, Micah replies. *No, that is not at all the truth. This is not trivial. It is the most real, the most challenging. People create atrocities because they disconnect from their souls.*

I don't understand. I say. *Am I really here? In the spirit world? Am I dead?*

People die randomly all the time. Could it be I had a brain aneurism or something?

You have to go now. Micah says. *There's important work for you to do, but remember... remember you came into this life for a reason.*

I feel a shiver of tingles, running right though my ethereal light body, and I can't tell if it's in resonance to his words, or if it's because something is shifting... pulling me down... contracting.

Remember... Micah says as the weight and hardness pushes in on me. *Life is supposed to be fun – You enter into your earth reality for pleasure... for joy... for expansion... and for the contrast of things you **don't** want... because that shows you exactly what you **do** want...*

It all makes sense at this higher level, and yet it's so disconnected from my life. I feel the falling sensation. I'm condensing, contracting back towards the physical plane as Micah vanishes.

27
HELIO

Who the hell is this guy? He comes in when we're just about to leave – to get Mira to a hospital, walks in like he owns the place.

"Get out," I say. We don't have time for this.

"Helio," says Gino, and there's a warning in his voice and in his eyes that puts me on edge.

"The thug wants to protect the lady," the stranger says. "How honorable."

What the fuck is going on?

He pulls back his hood further to reveal blonde hair, and there's something familiar about him, but I can't quite put my finger on it.

"You might not know me," he says, looking from me to Elias. "But I think Gino does from our few in-person meetings… and she certainly knows who I am," he gestures to Mira. The pieces finally click together in my mind.

"Clifford Maxwell," Gino says, addressing the guy who I now realize is Mira's psycho ex… the guy we've been running from… the guy I've been wanting to punch.

"What is it you want from us?" Gino asks.

Clifford eyes us with a look of cunning satisfaction on his face, as if he's got us right where he wants us.

I don't fucking think so, buddy...

The rage burns through me white-hot. I thought I wanted to punch the guy when I knew he was following us, but seeing him here, right now, strutting around like a cock and making threatening small talk when we need to get Mira to a hospital… I'm fucking livid.

I lunge towards him, but he's quick. He takes a step sideways while reaching for something in his jacket pocket. I fall to the floor, and Clifford Maxwell points the gun first to my head and then to Mira's.

"Get back to where you were, cowboy, or she gets a bullet in the skull."

The chill in his voice says he means it. He's not scared, not even nervous. Just cold and calculated, as if he choreographed this whole thing.

I push myself up and get back to where I was standing just moments ago, close to Mira, but not close enough.

How the fuck did Mira marry this psychopath?

Clifford Maxwell struts around the boat, pacing, from side

to side, staying near the open door. It's like they say: *a good criminal always knows their escape route.*

"Now what am I going to do with you…?" he says. "You four have given me quite the run-around."

He sounds maniacal and I feel like we're in the part of the James Bond film where the master criminal is about to tell us all about his grand plan.

"I knew you were headed to Athens, of course. It wasn't hard to get that whore of a pilot to play ball…"

"But how…" Gino starts to ask and then shuts up. Maybe it's not worth the risk. Clifford Maxwell seems to enjoy the half question though. His eyes light up.

"How did I follow you out to this godforsaken peasant island in the middle of nowhere?" he says, "I'm glad you ask. You see, I had wondered if you'd be onto me. I know you're smart, Gino. You knew I was a risk – only someone who was a risk would go to the effort to send rose petals and a wedding ring to the woman who walked out on him five years ago."

"Only someone who's a…" I start.

"Helio," Gino says, quietly but urgently telling me I should shut the fuck up, and he's right. I know he's right. All my outburst does is earn me another point of the gun before it swings back to Mira.

"Keep your guard dog in line, Gino," Clifford Maxwell says.

"Anyway… where was I? Oh yes. It was easy to seduce Inara… hardly any challenge at all. She was glad to tell me where you were going, and she even managed to plant the tracking chip I gave her right on you, Gino."

Gino's eyes widen, "What?"

"On your jacket, I believe, or perhaps on your designer man-bag. I forget the details now… but it worked like a charm."

"So, you followed us here using a GPS tracker?" Gino asks.

For a moment, I wonder why he's so interested in these details when Mira's life is at stake, but then it dawns on me that he's trying to keep this psycho talking, because hopefully, the more talking he's doing the less shooting he'll be doing.

I try to think of some questions, but then I realize I can't think of any that aren't likely to get one of us shot, so I tell myself to shut the fuck up and leave this to the expert: Gino. He's always had a way with words.

I quickly glance over at Elias. Tears are streaming down his face. He's a sensitive guy; he has such a big caring heart that he sometimes makes me uncomfortable, but now I wish I could hug him, and I'm not a big hugger.

It looks like Mira's still out cold on the sofa. Hopefully, she's still breathing; hopefully, her heart is still beating; hopefully, whatever the fuck is happening with her is not life threatening.

"It was a clever plan," Clifford Maxwell said. "Don't you agree?"

It sounds like a trick question and it takes every ounce of self-control I have not to bite back.

"You certainly outsmarted me," Gino says. "I thought we were safe here. I had no idea you were following so close behind."

"Excellent," Clifford Maxwell says, "which means your security detail are still chasing the decoy I left in a hotel on the way back to Athens. I walked in the front door, booked a room, then threw on a hooded jacket from the coat-stand and walked straight out the back before anyone would notice."

He paces back and forth again, looking pleased with himself. I watch him closely, waiting for the opportunity I need – waiting for him to be distracted, so I can kick away the gun and smash his fucking head in.

"So, the only question remaining," he says, "...is whether I should shoot you now or take you further out to sea. I suppose I'll need to keep at least one of you alive to drive this boat as it's beyond my level of captaining interest. Under normal circumstances, I'd hire someone but I'm sure I can persuade one of you to do it for free."

He waves the gun around at us.

Gino clears his throat, "Helio is the only one of us who can drive this thing."

"Pity," Clifford Maxwell says. "I was hoping to shoot the great oaf first."

He talks about ending my life, as if it's a minor missed opportunity, like the last salmon salad has already been sold from the restaurant menu, and he'll have to have the venison instead.

It chills me to the bone knowing we are this close to death, but I'm even more worried about Mira. Clearly, he doesn't immediately want her dead, or he would have killed her already, but he doesn't care that she's passed out and unconscious either, in fact, it seems like he prefers it this way; there's no one here who really knows him, less complications.

He looks around the boat, "Not bad," he says, gesturing with the gun around at the wood-paneled walls. "This would make a nice champagne breakfast venue, maybe even a sunset cruise."

It's beyond belief that he could be contemplating minor corporate events at a time like this.

"We're trying to get Mira to a hospital," Elias says. "She passed out."

"I know," Clifford Maxwell says, and a fire ignites in his eyes. "I saw your perverted activities. I know she passed out while fucking all of you." He grins. "That was certainly a surprise I didn't count on."

A sound like a moan is coming from the direction of the sofa.

Mira is stirring.

Thank fuck, she's okay.

"And look, here's the little slut coming to. Looks like you dragged her all the way down here in the rain for nothing… well, nothing other than making my escape more feasible."

28
MIRA

It's like moving through dimensions – transported from the most beautiful heavenly dream straight into the most hellish nightmare.

We are back on the boat, and the storm is still raging outside. I can see the guys all around me, but there's fear in the air, and Cliff is standing there in front of us all with a gun, postulating in his arrogant manner.

I try to pinch myself to shake myself out of this surreal hell… only it's not a dream. It's real. I'm here on the couch, and Cliff really is here, and he really does have a gun.

"What did you do to me?" I ask, still feeling disorientated, but needing to know what the fuck is going on.

"Nothing, Mira," Cliff says. "I did everything *for* you – everything… I looked after your every need I bought you expensive clothing, jewelry… I fed and housed you for years.

And how do you repay my generosity? You walk out on me without so much as leaving a note."

"Why am I here?" I ask, still feeling disorientated.

"Oh... that... well," Cliff seems more interested in ranting about our failed marriage than he does about the present situation.

"You passed out, Mira," Elias says. I can tell he's trying to reassure me, but there's so much fear in his voice that it's only making me more terrified, which is even worse as Cliff points the gun in his direction.

"Don't speak out of turn!" Cliff yells. He pulls the trigger and Elias buckles over.

"No!"

"Shut up," Cliff says. "Or they all get bullets."

I'm paralyzed in shock and fear. Elias is bleeding, gasping. He grasps his arm... Hopefully, it's just his arm...

"You see, Mira – you see what your slutty behavior has gotten you?"

"Please," I beg. "Please stop."

"That's not what you said before when you were fucking all three of these brutes at the same time, was it, Mira? Oh yes... I saw you... and don't think for a minute that I'll let that go unpunished."

"But... how?" I ask. I'm hoping I can keep him talking. I'm hoping someone has a plan... that something will distract him and that we can catch him off-guard before he has the chance to do any more damage.

I risk another glance at Elias. His face is pale, and my heart breaks imagining life without him… *How could I cope? How could any of us…?*

"Little Mira… you act so innocent, when really, you're a raging slut… You women, you're all the same. Like I said to your harem here: it was easy to track you. I barely broke a sweat, even when I was fucking that tart of a pilot."

I knew it! Gino wasn't sure, but I knew Inara must have been the spy. This is hardly the time to say *I told you so.*

"I just don't understand, Cliff. Honestly, why are you doing this?" I ask. "Why do you care?"

"I only bothered with this whole thing," Cliff says, "… because you're mine, Mira. And I always get what's mine. I knew about you all – well before this, and I'm going to put a stop to all of it before it happens again."

"You know about the other lives," Gino says.

Of course… it was too much of a coincidence… the pieces start to click into place in my mind… *This is why Cliff is so obsessed with me… with us…*

"If that's what you want to call this limbo we are stuck in. Yes." Cliff holds back his head and laughs. "Why else do you think I invested in your shitty little business, in your fucking hippy commune retreat? I needed a way in. Oversight. Control… but then you throw your little investigation at me, Gino," Cliff says, pointing the gun at Gino's chest.

I hold my breath.

"You have no idea who you're messing with. You know damn well that little tart I fucked years ago will have no bearing on my future."

So, Cliff knows about the leverage Gino discovered, the under-aged girl… this is why he's so wound up.

"She begged me for it, obviously." Cliff says. "They all do, and I don't deny it felt good fucking her tight little virgin pussy… I do like them young."

Cliff smiles as if lost in his own psychotic rapey delusions of grandeur.

"You were young too, Mira." He says and grins, pointing the gun back in my direction. "I bet it kills your new boyfriends to know that I got there first. I got to deflower you this time. It was a gift from the gods, clearly, when my father's business partner introduced me to his daughter… you fell straight into my lap, straight onto my cock. I thought I had you this time…"

"But how did you know?" I ask, shuddering at how creepy it all seems now. I was so young, so innocent. I had no idea what a creep I was bedding… marrying. I knew he was cold and heartless, but I had nothing to compare it to… nothing like the love I've now known from each of my four soulmates… And that's exactly what it is… My heart catches in my throat. I've finally realized I'm in love, and I'm not about to lose the guys now.

Great fucking time to realize you're in love, Mira…

That's exactly what it is I feel for them… I've always felt for them… *soul love.* I think back to the transcendent experience I just had with Micah. Do I love him too? What was it he said about the things I don't want showing me a greater understanding about the things I do want? How can I connect that understanding to this hellish situation? *The internal reflects the external... maybe if I can get to a better place inside my head, I can figure out how to save us all...*

I try to calm myself, calm my voice, and I ask Cliff the question that's been on my mind. "How did you know about the past lives?" I ask.

"Don't ask too many questions, you little whore. You don't deserve my attention, and it's not going to buy you any time. I'm onto you and your tactics..."

My calm voice only seems to aggravate him more, but maybe that's still getting us somewhere... I flinch as Cliff points the gun at Helio, who looks as if he's about to burst with rage. He's clearly stronger than even I thought... My Helio, his gorgeous muscular chest, naked and gleaming with raindrops in the low light...

Even in this desperate situation, Helio is truly magnificent to behold – the way he's visibly shaking in anger, holding himself back because he wants nothing more right now than to beat the living daylights out of Cliff. Helio grunts under the effort of holding back his rage.

"You, fucking meatbag," Cliff says, gesturing at Helio. "Don't think I haven't forgotten the look on your fucking dumb face as my wife sucked your cock."

This is just what Cliff does: he breaks you down, finds your insecurities, reduces you to nothing. I don't care that he's demeaning me. I've had so much worse from him, over so many years that his words are the poison I'm immune to. I've built up a tolerance, but the guys haven't.

It's strange to see how easy it is for Cliff's words to strike their intended target. Helio is so much more than his muscle, but by the way his face crumples, Cliff knows he's found an insecurity, and it's one I wasn't fully aware of. Helio is wounded by a simple insult – it's shocking, and I recall one of our early conversations where I had implied something similar.

This is part of why Helio is always so guarded. He's always been judged as a dumb jock, as more brawn than brain, and even though he wants nothing more than to be the wild man that his soul longs to be, he still has this pressure to prove he's not just worthless brute force – that's why he went to university to study engineering. That's why he puts on a suit and ties his hair back and goes to corporate events, and why he's always been the hardest of my guys to get close to.

Cliff pauses for effect, enjoying his mental abuse, enjoying the effect he can have on people without so much as lifting a finger, except his fingers are still clasped around the gun; one is still resting on the trigger.

Other than the rain pattering outside, my heartbeat is the only thing I can hear; we could be a heartbeat away from losing each other again. That's all it will take.

"You're going to get your stupid, ugly, ass over to the cockpit. Get behind the wheel and get us out of here," Cliff says to Helio.

Helio nods. I can see there are a million other things he'd

rather do that all involve disarming Cliff and beating him to a pulp even though I've never seen him hurt a fly.

"Nobody else move," Cliff says, waving the gun around as if he's a conductor in an orchestra – as if it's a fucking magic wand – which, at the moment, it kind of is. "Or Mira gets a bullet in her brain – what little brains she has, anyway."

It's the same shit he pulled all through our whole relationship. I'm stupid, worthless… I'm the cruel one… unless I give him everything he wants.

It took years for me to undo the damage this asshole did to my self-esteem, and I'm not going to let him win. *No. Never again.*

I never stood up to Cliff – not when we were married – not even after I left. I never had the guts or the self-worth… but it turns out I do now.

"Cliff… stop," I say.

"Shut up, Mira." He says, nonchalantly. "This is not the time to find your fucking voice. One more word from you and it's all over for Donatello over there." He gestures at Elias.

My gut tightens as I sneak another glance at Elias, who is still crumpled over with his eyes closed, clearly in pain.

Helio does as he's told, walking slowly over to the cockpit. No one speaks. No one moves.

There's a thud outside, and Cliff glances in its direction, but keeps the gun pointed at my chest.

Nothing is visible in the darkness, and he clearly decides there's nothing of interest out there – no one to interrupt his plan, whatever evil thing he's planning on doing now… but something about the sound gives me hope. Maybe someone was watching. Maybe they saw the danger and are on their way to call the local constable.

I'm grasping at straws because I'm desperate for a miracle.

"Get us out of here now!" Cliff yells. Helio gets the boat moving, and we accelerate out of the port and into deeper and deeper water, further and further away from the safety of the shore and all the other options for escape.

Fuck. Fuck. Fuck. I've lost control of my calm... we've all lost control.

I risk another glance over at Elias. It looks as though he's about to pass out from all the blood loss... My guess is, he doesn't have much time left.

"Now... let me think," Cliff says. "No one interrupt. I have to work this out... I need the meatbag to drive the boat – but I can eliminate... you," he says, pointing the gun towards Elias. "And I guess I have no use for Gino any more either... It's a shame. I was rather enjoying our business relationship. Too bad I didn't sell my stocks before the CEO went missing mysteriously at sea..."

I can't help it. I let out a sob.

"Quiet, Mira!" Cliff yells, pointing the gun back at me.

I see him for what he is: a child – a mini dictator. Someone who wants an army, but has to make do with hired thugs and weapons. Only, he didn't bring any of his goons with him. That means, this is personal for him. So personal he's left himself vulnerable. All it will take is one misstep.

He paces around the cabin. "That's it," he says, after a while.

"Genius... yes. We will head out to sea. And Meatbag is going to dump the bodies there... I'll still need him for a little while, just to get back to shore, and then I'll have to dispose of him myself. So, Mira... I'll have to keep you alive a little bit longer, just to make sure I have the most leverage... but Gino, I'm afraid, it's time to say goodbye."

Cliff points the gun directly at Gino's chest.

"No!" I cry, leaping up off the sofa. I throw myself in the way of Cliff's aim.

Out of the corner of my eye, I see the dark shape quick as lightning emerge from the door and barrel right into Cliff. There's a scuffle, confusion, fear, panic.

The gun goes off. The sound is still ringing in my ear as I hit the floor. I close my eyes, trying to embody Micah's advice. I've never been big on prayer, but right now I'm desperate. I pray to any powers that exist... I pray to Micah... I pray for whatever internal transformation I need to change the external outcome.

I hear a groan.

I check myself, taking stock of my body.

I'm fine.

I look towards Gino. His facial expression is one of shock, but he's alive... not in pain. I turn back in the direction of the scuffle, hearing moans and thuds. Helio is pinning Cliff to the ground effortlessly, and the other figure reaches down to wrestle the gun out of his hand. As he straightens up to his full height, I recognize him even though I've never ever seen him in anything as casual the black hoodie and jeans he's wearing.

"Theo!"

Theo is somehow here – the miracle I was praying for. He's standing over Helio and Cliff. He's looking across at me. There's an expression of relief on his face.

I let out a deep breath I didn't realize I was holding. I have so many questions, but they can wait. I turn towards Elias. Gino has clearly had the same thought. He's already checking for a pulse.

"He's still alive," Gino says.

Thank the gods.

"But it looks like he's lost a lot of blood," Gino continues. We have to get him to a hospital.

The next half an hour goes past in a blur. Theo finds some rope and helps Helio to restrain Cliff, who, after recovering from the shock of losing control of the entire situation, starts yelling and swearing so much that I'm relieved when Theo gags him. The muffled sounds are much easier to bear.

Helio drives the boat as quickly as possible towards mainland Greece. Meanwhile, Gino tears strips off his own designer shirt to stem Elias's bleeding.

Elias is fading in and out of consciousness, and in one particularly lucid moment, he laughs and tells Gino, "Maybe you should have been the doctor."

It melts my heart watching them; I can feel the connection between them and I'm praying to any god or higher power that will listen that Elias survives this; because Gino needs him, and I need him… we all need him.

I stand up and walk towards Theo. I'm a mess, but so is he,

and he doesn't seem to care. He opens his arms for me, and I fall into them.

"Thank you," I say. "You saved us... but how...?"

"Gino kept me updated, using out encrypted messenger program." he replies.

I look over towards Gino. *Of course, he did...*

"I wanted someone to know where we were headed," Gino says. "Someone I could trust to find us in case things went wrong."

"But how did you get here so fast?" I ask Theo, leaning deeper into him, inhaling his scent, his cologne, the one that smells like expensive leather and dark chocolate.

"As soon as Gino notified me that Clifford Maxwell was following you in Athens, I caught the first plane over," Theo says. "It was too much of a risk... I've heard rumors about this guy." He gestures in Cliff's direction. "In the business world, they say he's ruthless. And after the packages he kept sending you, Mira... I knew you weren't safe with him on your trail like that."

"Amazing... that you could find us all the way out here."

"Gino sent me co-ordinates when the boat moored," Theo says. "It was dark by the time I arrived, and I had not received any other messages from Gino, so I waited. I was about to give up and go to sleep on the hired launch, and then I saw you – saw the guys carrying you down. I was worried, of course. I would have run straight over to see how I could help, but then I saw him... Even in the dark. I knew it could only be him, so I crept over here, as quietly as I could. I was waiting for the right moment... for Cliff to let his guard down. I watched from outside, and then I got on board, just in time – before you left the port."

"That thud outside," I say. "That was you."

Theo nods. "I thought I might have blown my own cover tripping like that. I stayed completely still and listened until I knew there was no more time to lose. I had to act."

"Thank heavens, you did," I say.

The relief and tiredness suddenly catch up with me, and I have to lie down. I only close my eyes for a minute, and when I open them again, there are bright city lights and sirens. We are in a different world. The police are here. Of course, Gino had the foresight to call them before we even got near the mainland.

Elias is being taken into an ambulance, and Gino is going with him. Cliff is being untied by the police and handcuffed instead. There's another ambulance for me, but I'm sure I don't need it. "I'm fine," I tell them. I feel amazing. Really. They don't believe me, so I end up with Theo and Helio and the medic, crammed into the back of an ambulance... and the good thing about this is that we're going to the same hospital that Elias and Gino are headed to. We'll all be together...

Those are my last thoughts as everything fades to white again.

29
MIRA

It's a few days before everything is sorted and we can leave Athens. The doctors seemed mildly concerned about my 'fainting spells', but all my test results came back normal. I'm totally fine, if a bit exhausted from everything we've been through.

More importantly, Elias recovers well, with the help of a blood transfusion and a few stitches in his arm.

My residency permit comes through in less than 48 hours after the forms were lodged, thanks to Gino being a communications genius, so as soon as Elias can check out of the hospital, the five of us are on a plane, taking up most of the first-class cabin, heading back to Barcelona.

* * *

As we pull in through the front gates, I feel a deep sense of relief, a peacefulness, and a twinge of emotional significance from the sense of coming home. It's not a feeling I experienced much when I was younger, when home was a shiny, immaculate prison with either my father or Cliff as jailer. My shitty flat was a whole lot better, but nothing compared to this.

I can't wait to get back to my apartment and then continue plotting my nefarious plans to get all the guys into bed with me *at the same time...* Theo has been the missing link so far, but I'm working on him... wearing him down with my charm and wit and flirtatious overtures.

As we stumble in through the main entrance, Marina has a look of surprise on her face.

"You're back!"

She's clearly delighted to see us, and then her smile curves into a slight frown of concentration.

"A guest just arrived for you, Mira," she says.

"What?"

My heart leaps into my throat... *I didn't think the police or the courts would be able to hold Cliff forever, but surely he'd be locked up for longer than this over charges as serious as abduction and attempted murder...*

"Only ten minutes ago." Marina says, clearly concerned about my reaction based on the look on my face. "I told her you were away, but she insisted she'd wait for you."

"Wait... she?"

"Yes... should I send her away?" Marina asks just as a very familiar someone walks through the doors of the adjoining room.

"Lana!"

"I'm so glad to see you!" Lana says, running up and throwing her arms around me.

"But how did you get here?" I ask.

"It's a long story," Lana replies, and her face creases in worry. "There's something I need to tell you."

A NOTE FROM THE AUTHOR

Thank you for reading my book! If you want to find out what happens next you can order book 4: The Sound of Rain and Passion!

If you'd like to be emailed when I release my next book, you can sign up for my reader list.

Please consider leaving a review. I always appreciate reviews and seeing what readers have to say!

ABOUT THE AUTHOR

Lacuna Reid writes both fantasy and contemporary romance with a paranormal twist. She lives in beautiful New Zealand, where she enjoys writing books over a cup of earl grey tea or a glass of rosé wine, and eating all the delicious foods! She loves learning and has studied herbalism and completed a diploma in hypnotherapy. She's also a total astrology geek! Follow Lacuna on social media to see what she's up to.

Made in the USA
Columbia, SC
26 September 2021